These ~~~~
and they ~~~~
the distri~~ ~~~~~~~ ~~~~~

"You think I don't know that?" Jake knew he was beginning to sound aggravated. "I've been involved in this for months. I've seen what they can do." His brother Adam was still recovering from being shot months ago.

"I have, too." Rose sounded grim. "I just don't want to see any more of this close to home. Don't forget you've got one of my favorite cousins working for you, mister. I want to keep her in one piece."

"No need to worry on that score. I wouldn't let anybody touch Holly. If I lost her, the office would fall apart."

* * *

FAITH ON THE LINE:
Two powerful families wage war on evil…and find love.

RELIGIOUS

ROMANCE

Books by Lynn Bulock

Love Inspired

Gifts of Grace #80
Looking for Miracles #97
Walls of Jericho #125
The Prodigal's Return #144
Change of the Heart #181
The Harbor of His Arms #204
Protecting Holly #279

LYNN BULOCK

has been writing since fourth grade and published in various fields for over twenty years. Her first romantic novel came out in 1989. Her Steeple Hill Café mystery LOVE THE SINNER is a May 2005 release. She lives near Los Angeles, California, with her husband and sons.

PROTECTING HOLLY

LYNN BULOCK

Steeple
Hill®

Published by Steeple Hill Books™

To Joe, always

Special thanks and acknowledgment are given to Lynn Bulock for her contribution to the FAITH ON THE LINE series.

STEEPLE HILL BOOKS

Steeple
Hill®

ISBN 0-373-87289-5

PROTECTING HOLLY

www.SteepleHill.com

Printed in U.S.A.

Keep me, O LORD, from the hands
of the wicked; protect me from men
of violence who plan to trip my feet.

—*Psalms* 140:4

Cast of Characters

Jake Montgomery—Someone was out to make sure the FBI agent never finished decoding Alistair Barclay's secret files.

Holly Vance—She'd loved her boss in silence for years, but would the traumatic past she'd buried keep them apart?

Alistair Barclay—The former hotel tycoon was going down for numerous crimes. Would Jake be able to connect him with Baltasar Escalante and the Diablo crime syndicate?

Maxwell Vance—The former CIA agent has a vested interest in the case: keeping his three sons out of the line of fire.

Peter Vance—He was one of the last ones to see Escalante alive…and one of the many on hand to testify against Barclay.

Chapter One

"You are so lucky." Sara Phelps straightened a stack of papers fresh from the copier. "You know that everybody else in the Colorado Springs office wants your job, don't you?"

Holly Vance waved a hand in her friend's direction. She couldn't imagine what Sara said being true. "That has to be an exaggeration, Sara. For one thing, 'everybody' in this office would only mean about three other people. And why would they want my job, anyway? I do the same things the rest of the assistants here do."

When Holly told friends she worked for the FBI, they all thought her job must be terribly fascinating. She had to burst their bubble fairly frequently on that little fantasy. For the most part, working for the resident agency of the FBI in Colorado Springs was a lot like working for any other government office. The idea of the work might sound interesting to an outsider, but the day-to-day routine was just that most of the time…routine.

Holly knew that she went to work in a regular office building like most of the population. She spent hours on the computer and a lot of time just like this, queuing up for one of the printers or copiers in the suite of offices, processing a document for her boss, Jake Montgomery. The khakis and sweater she wore on her slender frame weren't any different from the work outfits of any of her friends. Television, she decided, had overplayed the image of working for the Federal Bureau of Investigation.

Of course there was the fact that Jake could easily have played one of those TV FBI agents. His dark-blond good looks would make him a casting director's dream. But Holly knew that personally, *she'd* never make the cut on a television casting call, and neither would most of the people working in the Colorado Springs office.

Sara leaned on the side of the copier and sighed. Holly thought she looked much younger than twenty-five some days, with her spiky hair and clothing choices that always skated to the limit of what the bureau would allow its support personnel to wear. Today her slacks were gray pinstripe, but tailored in such a way that one wrong move would have exposed the tattoo that Holly knew covered the small of her friend's back. Watching Sara made her feel even older than the twenty-nine she was, and like a much more seasoned veteran of the bureau.

"Maybe you do the same things," Sara said, waggling deep burgundy polished nails. "But consider how you do them, and who you get to do them for. If either of the special agents I worked with were half as cool as Jake Montgomery, I'd be so happy."

Holly picked her own documents out of the print tray. She hardly knew what to say to Sara. Jake probably did seem like the coolest guy in the Colorado Springs office. With his specialization in computers, he didn't have some of the same restrictions or duties as the other special agents, so he was a little more fascinating than the rest of the professionals on staff. On top of that, he was a Colorado Springs native with plenty of history behind him. Most of the other agents were transplants from somewhere else, some still serving their first assignment probationary period with the bureau.

Still, it was hard to believe that working for Jake could be perceived as that big a plum. Colorado Springs wasn't even that big an FBI office to begin with. There were only eleven people in the FBI offices in the brick building tucked away on a downtown side street, and six of those people were support staff like her, or other non-agent personnel.

"So you think working for Mr. Montgomery would be a cool thing, huh?" He might look handsome and glamorous, but Holly wondered how Sara would handle Jake's constant flights into programming language. Most of it didn't begin to resemble English when he started discussing the complex computer work that he did. Of course, most of it made sense to her, because she'd been assisting him for two years now. And the lingo wasn't even the most challenging part of working with Jake.

Sara wrinkled her nose. "Well, usually. Not right now, though. I have a life already."

Holly didn't even have to ask what that reference was about. "I know. And thanks so much for reminding me that I don't have one."

Sara's cheeks colored. "Hey, Holly, I didn't say that."

Holly smiled. "It probably wasn't even what you meant. But if Jake really has to find all that information on the computers they took in the drug raid, and find it before the trial starts later this month, neither of us is going to have a life until it's finished. And we all know that's going to be harder on my boss than it is on me."

Any casual reader of the *Colorado Springs Sentinel*'s society pages could tell you that normally, Jake Montgomery had a life. He had, in fact, one of the most glamorous and best documented lives in Colorado Springs. As the mayor's son and one of the most eligible bachelors in the city, there always seemed to be pictures of Jake's handsome face in the paper, getting out of his bright-red Viper for a charity event, or partying in a well-tailored tuxedo somewhere.

Holly wondered how much of that would go by the wayside between now and Alistair Barclay's trial. The shady hotel tycoon was accused of everything from racketeering to running the biggest drug ring the city had seen in over a decade.

The FBI had given Jake the job of going over the computer files taken from Baltasar Escalante, head of the Venezuelan crime family Barclay had been accused of working for, in order to nail down Barclay's prosecution. From what little her boss had told her, they were going to be working some unbelievable hours until all the information was deciphered. That didn't really go along with Jake's usual round of holiday parties and charity events right before Christmas.

It was hard for Holly to feel sorry for him on that score. If anyone had asked her—which no one was going to—she would have said that Jake Montgomery spent too much time flitting from one party to the next with a bevy of escorts. Surely at almost thirty-five he was getting ready to settle down.

"Hey, you still in there?" Sara teased, waving a hand near Holly's face.

Okay, so maybe thinking about her good-looking boss led to a little daydreaming once in a while. Holly gave a wry grin. "Sure am. Just thinking about all the stuff I'm going to be doing around here in the next month. Of course, I might be talked into trading jobs with someone who only had to organize the office party and the gift exchange on top of a normal schedule."

Sara shook her head emphatically. "No way. Like I said, Holly, most of the time I envy you because you work for Jake Montgomery. Now isn't most of the time."

"That's true." Holly knew what Sara's answer would be even before she gave it. And in truth, that was the only reason that Holly offered to switch jobs with her friend, even in fun. Because when it came down to it, Holly Vance knew that her time every day with Jake was what kept her going. Prayer and her faith held her together through the dark nights, and working with Jake kept her going through the long days.

No matter how many hours of challenging work she put in, she wouldn't trade for another job. There were cushier jobs out there, and there were better paying jobs out there, but none of them had the fringe benefit of working side by side with Jake eight to ten hours a day. There wasn't a benefits package out there anyplace that could take the place of watching her handsome boss do what he was best at.

Holly finished her last bit of copying. "Tell you what. I'll ask you again when this trial is over some time in January. Once you've watched Mr. Montgomery pace around snarling for a couple weeks trying to decipher all those files, we'll see if you still want to trade jobs." It was an easy offer to make. Jake might be charming to look at, but he growled like a tawny tiger when things didn't go his way.

Sara's smile was a little faded. "Sure." She picked up her papers and headed toward her office down the hall. "But for now I better get back to planning the party."

For a moment Holly wished that Christmas parties were all she was planning. But she already had an idea how much this prosecution meant to Jake, and to so many other people she knew. This might not be the most festive Christmas she ever had, but if the government won its case against Alistair Barclay, there would be plenty to celebrate later.

"You want this guy as badly as I do." There was a note of surprise in Rose D'Arcy's voice. The petite assistant district attorney seemed to be taking a fresh look at Jake. It always amused Jake that one of the toughest legal pit bulls in the county came packaged in this tiny redheaded person.

"Why do you look so surprised? Thanks to him and his crew I could have lost my brother. I know it's not like Barclay pulled the trigger, but the man who shot Adam was working for him as much as he was anybody."

Rose shrugged. "Him and Baltasar Escalante. But we can't put Escalante on trial yet."

"Not until somebody finds him. And I don't expect that to happen anytime soon." Escalante, the drug lord who made the activities of some of the sleaziest crooks in Colorado Springs possible, had managed to escape during the raids on his Venezuelan compound. "But at least Peter Vance got the goods on him."

"Yeah, he did. With the two of you involved, this has been a great pretrial. He's a friend of yours, isn't he?"

"My best friend, from way back. Adam wasn't the only one who'd risked his life taking on the La Mano Oscura drug ring. Peter built this case for years before you and I got hold of it."

Jake tapped a stack of computer disks with a slim finger. "Now if I can just tie all this back to Barclay and find the corresponding info on his computer, at least we can put him away for a few decades. And maybe that will give us the time to find Escalante and put him away, too."

"Yeah, well that's possible. But I'm not here to congratulate you on helping us to convict Barclay, even though I'll be cheering you every step of the way. I'm here to remind you to be even more careful than usual while you do it."

"That will be hard to do." Jake tried to sound more cool and calm than he felt. "I'm always careful to a fault." For a change the work-issue sidearm in his shoulder holster felt like a comfort instead of an annoyance.

"Says the man who has paid so many moving violation tickets he's paid for his own Colorado Springs patrol car." Rose's grin was wolfish.

"It can't be that high. Maybe a scooter by now. Or part of the winter feed for one of the horses. But not a whole patrol car yet. It's the car, anyway. A red Viper just screams 'ticket me,'" Jake grumbled. "And the Escalade isn't any more cop friendly. When I switch over to that when winter starts, it's just as bad."

"You could drive something more sedate." Rose's expression told Jake she knew that wasn't going to happen. "Parking tickets aside, I know you're a pretty safe guy for being FBI. But I don't trust any of these guys that are still out on the street. Escalante may have vanished, but a lot of money vanished with him. And it would be in his best interests if Barclay walked. Or even better, if he died quickly and quietly and the evidence never materialized."

Jake waved a hand in dismissal. "Not possible. You and your boss already have plenty of evidence to convict Barclay and put him away for longer than his natural life expectancy. And I know everybody's watching him like a hawk after what happened to that doctor." They might be months further along in this process if Escalante hadn't gotten to his plant within Doctors Without Borders so quickly. After that jail-house murder, nobody was leaving Barclay alone for a moment.

"It's still not enough to tie him to Escalante, which is just the way everyone would like it. I mean it, Jake. These guys play rough, and they play for keeps."

"You think I don't know that?" Jake knew he was beginning to sound aggravated. "I've been involved in this for months. I've seen what they can do." Adam was still recovering from being shot months ago during a drug robbery at the Venezuelan clinic he'd been working in for Doctors Without Borders.

"I have, too." Rose sounded grim. "I just don't want to see any more of it this close to home. Don't forget you've got one of my favorite cousins working for you, mister. I want her kept in one piece."

Jake had to think about that one a minute. This tiny terror was related to Holly? Of course. When she wagged her finger in his face as she was doing now, she looked just like her aunt, Holly's mother. Marilyn D'Arcy Vance had terrorized a couple generations of Colorado Springs high schoolers before moving on to another job.

"Holly? No need to worry on that score. I wouldn't let anybody touch Holly. If I lost her, the office would fall apart."

Rose grimaced, wrinkling her pug nose. "Glad to know you're so fond of her on such a personal basis, Jake."

Jake shrugged. "Dates are easy to get. But a good assistant…I couldn't replace her if I tried."

"See that you don't have to. I'm holding you personally responsible for her safety, as well as your own. The task force is already spread pretty thin cleaning up the loose ends of Diablo."

Jake knew there were still branches of the crime syndicate active in and around Colorado Springs. The task force didn't need to worry about him as well. "We'll be okay. Go get some rest. Go home and have dinner with your feet up."

Rose made a most unladylike noise in dismissal of that comment. "Right, like that's going to happen anytime the rest of this year. Maybe after the trial."

The two said their goodbyes and Jake went back to his desk. There was still plenty to do in order to nail Alistair Barclay. It was a good thing he didn't have one particular woman in his life right now, because if he had, she would be plenty peeved at him. Rose was right. Cracking this case was going to take every waking hour for the next few weeks.

On Wednesday Holly got to work at seven-thirty in the morning, sure that she would have a clean desk for a change. There was plenty of space in the parking garage this early for her Jeep, and the roads were clear of the light snow that had fallen the previous day.

She'd stayed until seven the night before, leaving only when Jake promised that he was right behind her on the way out. One look at her work station told her that was a promise he hadn't kept. There were three files with notes jotted in his awful handwriting all over the margins, and at least half a dozen sticky notes on the papers and her computer screen.

Sighing, she hung her coat on the rack, put down her coffee and started deciphering the notes. The most interesting said "Book us a working lunch at the Stagecoach."

Jake hardly ever took her out to lunch unless he needed something special from her. Given the nature of the case he was working on, she could only imagine what kind of favors he was going to ask this time. She hoped it wasn't canceling all his dates to the various charity balls and benefit parties this holiday season. Or ordering flowers as an apology for all his stood-up partners for those functions. She could handle a lot working for Jake, but some things were beyond her comfort level.

Still, she wouldn't turn down going to the Stagecoach Café for lunch and sampling some of her aunt Lidia's marvelous cooking. It was just cold enough this morning to hope that Lidia had made minestrone soup *and* chili to counteract the chill in the air.

By the time Jake came in at eight, Holly had dealt with all the sticky notes except one, and checked her e-mail for bureau updates and other business. Coffee was steaming in a thermal carafe and Jake's blinds were open precisely enough to let the morning sun in without any glare on his computer screen, just the way he liked it.

Of course he would never notice any of that. Whistling, her handsome boss hung his wool topcoat on the coat rack and went straight for the coffee, where his favorite Colorado State Rams mug sat next to the carafe, upside down and spotless.

"Good morning, Holly." Her heart leaped at the sight of him, as it did most mornings. By now Holly knew she was practiced enough at keeping her outside appearance calm that Jake never knew how he affected her. His charcoal suit fit like no off-the-rack garment ever could, and his dark-blond hair was cut just perfectly. She was glad to see that, because it was hard to guess when he might get time for a haircut during this case.

"Morning, Jake." She waved the stack of sticky notes she'd piled up. "What happened to leaving here early enough to go by the Toys for Tots drive at your dad's office?" Mayor Montgomery had kicked off the local drive with a well-publicized cookies and cocoa party, complete with Santa Claus in attendance. Holly had seen it on the local news last night, but Jake had been conspicuous in his absence.

Jake grimaced, making the laugh lines around his blue eyes crinkle. "So I didn't quite get there on time. I managed to duck in before Santa left, though. And I brought lots of cool toys, too."

"I'll just bet. All of them had wheels, didn't they?" After two years of being in this office, Holly knew that her boss's weaknesses were few. He was a hard-working guy who may have gone to a lot of parties, but was seldom, if ever, photographed holding anything stronger than a cola. Cars, however, were another matter.

Jake grinned. "They might have had. Are we on for lunch?"

"We are. Twelve-thirty at your favorite table." Jake was at the Stagecoach Café so often he had his own spot near the fireplace in the winter, and a prime corner on the patio in the summer. Of course it wasn't usually Holly who was there with him, even though she often made the reservations.

No, Jake's lunch companions at the Stagecoach Café were normally beautiful young women from the high society of Colorado Springs, and hardly ever the same one twice. Holly often wondered if it aggravated Jake's mother as much as it aggravated her that the man flitted from one woman to the next at a speed faster than the processors in his computer.

No matter who else it bothered, his activity didn't seem to bother Jake. He looked over the messages Holly had already started collecting in the half hour she'd been in and gave a low growl. "Okay, well, I probably won't be out here much before lunch. Fend off all calls and visitors unless they're family. And I mean yours, not mine."

"What?" Jake didn't often confuse her, but he was doing so now.

Jake's smile made the laugh lines around his eyes crinkle a little more, making Holly's heart race a little faster. "You haven't gotten through all your e-mail, I see. My new 'calls allowed' list includes nobody besides Rose D'Arcy and the Vance family, specifically Maxwell, Travis, Peter and Sam." Holly understood why her cousin Rose topped the list, as assistant district attorney. But it was odd to have Uncle Max and all three of her male cousins make up the rest of that list.

"Well, at least my family will know where I am and what I'm doing." Holly laughed. "Nobody can grouse when they don't get a Christmas card from *me* this year."

She wasn't about to tell Jake that nobody ever got a Christmas card from her except a few of the people she volunteered with at the Galilee Women's Shelter. By the time she was done sending out all the business-oriented ones from the office most years,

she was tired of looking at them. And this year nobody was going to get those, either.

"Hey, there are always fruitcakes." That was what
made working with Jake so much fun. He had a quick
wit and sharp sense of humor. "No absolutely necessary meetings from inside today?"

Holly shook her head. "I made sure you were off
the list for anything but the highest alert levels from
the regional field office or Washington. You should
be able to make Barclay your only priority for as long
as it takes."

"Ah, Holly, you're too good to me." She wasn't
sure what made her smile back so quickly—the
words or the smile that went with them. Both made
her feel just a little more inclined toward taking care
of Jake Montgomery.

His door closed and Holly stared at it with a sigh.
What would be more dangerous…Jake remaining
happily oblivious about how much she cared for him,
or Jake knowing just how much she cared? Either one
broke her heart. In the long run, she decided, going
back to her cooling coffee and insistent computer
screen, having Jake know she cared would be even
more dangerous. Because there was no way there
could ever be anything between her and a man like
Jake Montgomery.

Four hours later Holly was ready to wring her
boss's gorgeous neck. "For a man who doesn't want

to be disturbed, you sure are disturbing me plenty," she said, coming into the office with his latest request off the shared printer down the hall. He had his own printer in the office, but it wasn't of the quality of the networked one, nor could it handle some of the bigger demands he put on it. So Holly was the one bouncing up and down getting what he'd ordered.

This was on top of fending off all the calls from everyone who was sure Jake wanted to talk to them and the requests for other computer work from bureau personnel around the state who kept getting put on Jake's ever growing waiting list. By the time he finished up Barclay's evidence, he was going to have enough other cases to keep him busy until Memorial Day of next year, Holly was sure. And lucky her, she would be the one placating all those people while they groused about why Jake hadn't gotten back to them yesterday.

Jake glanced over the documents she brought in. "Thanks. There's got to be a pattern in this someplace. Maybe if I rearrange it and print it out a couple more times I'll have the basis to his algorithm."

His harried comment told her that Jake was still trying to crack the passwords to get into Barclay's private files. More than likely, there were passwords on top of passwords. Jake would be a bear to be around until he'd found at least one or two levels of them. After a moment of her standing in front of the desk, Jake looked up again. "Something else?"

"We had a lunch date at twelve-thirty, remember?"

Startled, he looked at his watch. "It can't be that late. But it is." He stood, setting the papers aside. "Right. Want to ride with me?"

"Sure. Let me get my purse and I'll be ready to go. But I'm not using my 'in' with the police department to get you out of any speeding tickets."

Jake grinned. "You won't have to. I think Sam told them to lay off me for the minor stuff as long as I'm working for the task force," he said with a teasing grin. "Besides, it's lunch hour in the middle of the city. I can't go fast enough anyplace to get a ticket."

He was right there. The short trip to the Stagecoach Café only took about ten minutes anyway, and before they knew it Jake and Holly were sitting beside the crackling fire, looking at the specials. She was happy to see that Aunt Lidia had put chili on the menu today, along with her famous minestrone. A baked potato loaded with Lidia's chili was just the thing to take the chill off the day. Holly didn't have to look any further on the menu.

They ordered and sat waiting for their food. Jake pulled out his leather-bound PDA, turning it on and looking over at Holly. "We've been working together too long for me to pull one over on you."

"No such thing as a free lunch," Holly said with a sigh. "What's this one going to cost me?"

"Not as much as you might think. Just a little bit

of Christmas shopping. You work with the shelter my mom's so involved in, don't you?"

She was surprised he'd noticed, even at the gala in October. "Galilee? Sure I do." It was on the tip of her tongue to ask what that had to do with anything, but she held off. Jake never kept her in suspense long.

"I never know what to get Mom for Christmas. It's the one gift I usually stew over all of December and frankly this year I don't have the time. I figured maybe you could figure out something the shelter needs and arrange to get it done in her name."

He told her what her budget was and Holly's eyes widened. She didn't spend that much on her own mom if she added up gifts for a decade. But then, she wasn't a Montgomery, either.

Their food came, and the waitress served it quickly and left. Holly was ready to ask him what else he needed done when a silky voice greeted him someplace close behind her. "Jake, fancy seeing you here. Please, don't get up."

The tone of the woman's voice said she didn't mean that, but Jake took her at her word. Holly looked back at the petite blonde, dressed for the Colorado winter in a ridiculously formfitting leather jacket with fur trim. It was the kind of "fun" coat that only someone with as much money as the Montgomerys, and far less common sense, would own.

"Zoe Taylor, Holly Vance. Holly's my assistant,

Zoe." The woman's speculating look eased a little. Not that Holly could imagine this woman seeing her as a threat.

"Ah. Business lunch?"

"The first of many, I'm afraid. Which is why I left that message on your machine last night canceling our date for the mayor's Christmas party."

Zoe's full pink lips drew into a pout. "I heard it, and I think you're mean, Jake. How on earth do you think I'll get someone else to go with me at this late date? You can't possibly cancel."

"I can, I'm afraid. Already have if you remember. Why don't you give my cousin Brendan a call, see what he's doing? Or if you like, I could do it for you…"

Zoe backed off in horror. "No, that won't be necessary. I can still get my own dates to charity functions. I'll see you later, Jake."

After Zoe left, Holly and Jake finished their meal in relative silence and before she knew it, Holly was back in the front passenger seat of the red Escalade. It was a reminder of the passing seasons that Jake had garaged his sports car for the winter and brought out the heavier vehicle, still the same deep, glossy red as the Viper. "Okay, now where are we going?" she asked as Jake pulled out of the restaurant parking lot in the opposite direction she expected.

"Courthouse. I need to get one more thing from

Rose." Jake was silent for two blocks, whistling thinly through his teeth.

"That's odd," he blurted, making the turn for the courthouse's underground garage.

"What is it?" It was a rare thing for Holly to see her boss agitated over something while driving.

"I thought for a minute…" Jake trailed off, checking frequently in the rearview mirror. "No, must have been mistaken. There are so many dark-blue SUVs around here. I can't have really seen the same one three times in the course of one afternoon."

Holly was inclined to agree with him. But if she did, what was making the hair on the back of her neck underneath the tight dark-brown French braid start to prickle in apprehension?

Chapter Two

"Are you still here?" Sara stood in the doorway to Holly's office, her coat on and a scarf wound around her neck.

Holly looked up, startled. "Of course I am. Are you leaving early? You have a doctor's appointment or something?"

Sara laughed. "Early? Not exactly. It's five-thirty, my regular time to head out of here."

Holly looked at her watch, stunned. "You're kidding. We missed lunch again. I'm going to have to start setting an alarm clock or something. Maybe I'll send out for dinner, anyway."

Sara started unzipping her coat and walked into the office. *Great,* Holly thought, *here comes a lecture.*

Sara didn't disappoint her. "I know you're on a big project, but girl, you have got to get a life. At least enough of one so that you don't come in here when it's barely light out every morning and leave after dark every day. When was the last time you saw sunlight? You look pale."

"Hey, I don't tan anyway. Not during the summer, or even on the ski slopes. So that's not a good indicator of how often I'm outside," Holly argued. Maybe it would deflect Sara's question, because the real answer was almost embarrassing. In the week since she'd had lunch with Jake, the only daylight she'd seen on any day but Sunday had been driving to work in the morning.

Given his drive right now, she'd almost expected Jake to protest when she told him that she wouldn't be working Sundays no matter what happened. Instead he just nodded. "I expected that. In fact my mother would applaud. She's horrified that I'm not at least taking the time off on Sunday mornings to meet the rest of the family at Good Shepherd. Of course it isn't like I make it on a regular basis even when I'm not swamped."

Holly could have told him that without thinking much. She saw his parents virtually every Sunday, and Adam and his new bride Kate seemed to put in regular appearances since he'd begun to recuperate from his gunshot wound. Even his sister Colleen, jaded and busy newspaper reporter that she was, made it to church many Sundays. Holly held her tongue, knowing that adding to the complaints Jake was already hearing from his mother wasn't a good idea. She knew how little she heeded anybody who agreed with her own mother's nagging that she needed to get out more and do things with people. Why aggravate her boss, even if she agreed with his mother? A noise brought Holly back to the present.

Sara was still standing in front of the desk, tapping a foot and waiting for an answer. "Okay, I'll try to get out more. At least enough to see daylight once in a while, anyway. But it's not going to happen right away. There's just too much to do every day to get ready for this trial."

"It must be something. Even Jake Montgomery, champion workaholic, doesn't usually keep you here this many hours."

"I'm keeping myself here most of the time," Holly countered. It was true, mostly. Jake would have let her go home much earlier than she did, if he'd noticed that she was putting in the kind of hours she was. Of course he didn't notice much right now that wasn't related to Alistair Barclay's computer or the disks he'd gotten from the raid on the La Mano Oscura cartel. That much was obvious in the fact that he hadn't thought about lunch, or even coffee, for hours.

"You know, I'd better check on Jake, now that you mention it. He hasn't been out here in hours." Holly cast a worried glance at his door.

"Do that. And then go home." Sara looked as stern as a young woman in a fuzzy angora scarf could look.

"I will. Or at least get out of here pretty soon. There are all kinds of things I need to catch up on outside the office."

"I'll just bet. And only sixteen shopping days 'til Christmas," Sara piped up with a wicked grin.

Holly groaned. "Don't even remind me. Now go home yourself and let me check on Jake."

"Will do. See you in the morning, Holly. I know you'll be here when I get in. You always are."

She couldn't argue with Sara on that score either, Holly thought as she got up from her desk and crossed the room to Jake's door. She knocked softly, but there was no answer. "Jake? You there?"

He was there, propped straight up at his desk, all right. Hands on the keyboard, still sitting up in his chair, Jake Montgomery was asleep. Holly stifled a giggle. It was funny and painful at the same time, watching her boss dozing at his desk.

She walked up quietly and softly rested a hand on his shoulder. She didn't want to startle him too much. "Jake?" she called out quietly. Even that woke him quickly. He reared backwards, almost upsetting his chair.

"What?" Dazed, he shook his head. "Holly? Don't tell me I fell asleep."

"Sitting straight up. Jake, this has got to end. You

need a real night's sleep at home in bed. I need the same. And we both need a good, hot nutritious meal."

Jake recovered quickly from his nap. "Does this mean you're asking me out?"

"No." Her reaction was so quick, and so snappish, Holly even surprised herself. How could she react to Jake that way, of all people? "That is, I didn't mean to suggest that we have dinner together. Just that we both need a hot meal and plenty of rest."

"I understand. And you're right. Maybe if I just finish this one thing…"

Holly felt herself clucking like a mother hen. "Jake Montgomery, I've never crossed you in the two years I've worked here. But this time I'm going to. Neither of us will be worth anything to this investigation if we get sick and worn-out. And you're skating on thin ice, mister. Go home. Get some rest. Send out for a pizza, or Chinese or something. I know there's probably nothing worth eating in that bachelor loft you call home."

"You're right. I think there's a carton of orange juice, something that used to be cheese, and an almost empty mustard jar in the whole refrigerator. And don't even get me started on the pantry. If I had mice, they'd starve." Jake's grin was wry. "And you're right about going home for a change, too."

"I know I am. And this time I'm going to walk out with you to make sure you actually leave. You keep telling me you're going home at night and then you don't." Holly knew she sounded stern, but she'd learned from the best. Her mom had taught high school English for more than a dozen years before she'd become the receptionist at the *Sentinel*. Nobody could do stern like a high school English teacher. Jake was just lucky he wasn't chewing gum.

The next morning Holly took her time heading for the office for a change. It was what she'd "traded" Jake for by making him leave early the night before. "I'll go home now, and have a decent dinner on the way there, if you don't show up until at least nine tomorrow morning. Deal?" His blue eyes were sharp again after his little nap.

"Deal. I'll even make it ten." Holly hadn't told him that she'd spend the time before she came in lining up his mother's Christmas gift. If he thought she was actually doing something for herself, he'd be more tolerant of the late entry into the office. But if she spent all that time on herself, she'd feel worse, so this made more sense.

She knew from past experience that Jessica Mathers Vance would be at her desk fairly early most days, and she'd be the one to speak to about some kind of gift for the shelter to make in Liza Montgomery's name. Although what Liza hadn't already given the shelter, Holly couldn't imagine. In the time that

Holly had volunteered there, an anonymous benefactor had donated quite a bit over the years, and a few months ago the mayor's wife had quietly revealed herself to be that benefactor.

Still, it was good of Jake to actually realize how close the shelter was to his mother's heart, and to know that doing something for Galilee would make her happier than some more traditional Christmas present. Holly sighed. Her boss was thoughtful in many ways when he put his mind to it. The shame was that he didn't put his mind to it very often. When he had time to spend outside the office, he spent it socializing with a variety of lovely young ladies like Zoe.

Of course, she reflected, Jake was free to spend his time any way he liked. She just wished he didn't seem to like that empty party life so much. It wasn't as if drinking had any draw for him that Holly could see. And the "big money" aspect of that kind of social life didn't seem to interest him. What did pull Jake into that scene was the biggest mystery about the handsome, secretive man she worked with every day.

When Holly got to Jessica's office she was surprised to see it empty. It looked like Jessica had been there and just stepped down the hall for something, so Holly stood there by the doorway and waited for a minute.

Jessica's office was brighter than Holly remembered it. Looking around, she tried to decide what the difference was. There was a great photo of Sam, Jessica and her sweet daughter Amy on the desk. It must have been taken on their wedding day this last fall. All three were smiling broadly at whoever had taken the picture.

It wasn't just a photo or two that made the room brighter, though. It seemed a warmer, happier place than it ever had before. Of course, Holly hadn't been in here since Jessica had found her daughter after she'd disappeared, kidnapped by a baby-sitter. Nothing about Jessica's life had been particularly bright when she was looking for her daughter. Now that Amy was back and Jessica had married Sam, her life was so different.

As Holly stood lost in thought, praising God for the changes in her friend's life, Jessica hurried down the hall toward her. "Holly, good to see you. I hope you haven't just been standing here in the hallway very long." She motioned her into the office and they both sat down.

Holly waved away her concern. "Not long at all. Besides, I was enjoying looking at a desk where you can actually see the top of it."

Jessica laughed. "Ouch. I don't have to ask how things are going at work for you, then, do I?"

"Not exactly. Jake is working on stuff for Alistair Barclay's trial, and it's coming up soon. I guess that's partially why I'm here."

Jessica looked confused. "What does somebody as slimy as Barclay have to do with you being here?"

"Just his trial. It has us so busy, and Jake so completely swamped, that I came by to do two things. I need for you to take me off the volunteer schedule for a while until things get back to normal."

"I can pass that word on to Susan, the shelter's director. I hope this doesn't mean you'll miss the Christmas party."

"Not if I can help it. I can't make room for much on my schedule this month, but if I do anything, it will be the party here. It's always such a good time."

Holly had been volunteering at the shelter for most of the time she'd been back in Colorado Springs since leaving her job in Ohio. This was probably the fifth Christmas she'd been around the Galilee Women's Shelter, and she didn't have any intention of missing the best Christmas party in town. Mayor Montgomery might have a more elegant one, and Jake probably went to half a dozen most years that were flashier than this one, but nobody had one where more delighted kids squealed over their gifts.

"I really hope you can make it. This one is going to be such a special Christmas for me personally. Lots of firsts involved." Jessica's gray eyes shone with happiness.

"I guess so. I'll just have to make it here for that," Holly said. "And it ties in nicely with the other reason for my trip over here."

"Oh? If you're going off the volunteer schedule, it can't be an offer of help for the party."

"Not exactly. At least not from me. But Jake needs to get his mom a meaningful Christmas gift, and he thought that contributing money for something here would be the best thing to do. Once you mentioned the party, I thought maybe I'd ask if you needed any more funding for it."

"Always. Even with all the wonderful people like Liza Montgomery who give time and money to this place, there's always more that can be done." Jessica's normally smooth forehead wrinkled. "Especially since we were counting on one hundred thousand dollars from Mr. Barclay that turned out to be non-existent. We could hardly take money from him now. But maybe if you guys put people like him away, and others who help bring drugs into town, we'd have fewer clients to have to provide for in the first place."

"Wouldn't that be great?" Holly tried to imagine a world in which no woman felt the need to go to a place like Galilee. It was hard for her to do. Once her life had been sheltered enough that she hadn't known places like this existed. Now she'd seen enough of the outside world's ugliness, even before working for the FBI, that she knew just what some people were capable of. Silently, she thanked God that most people weren't capable of terrible evil.

"It would. And we can always pray for it to happen." In a flash, Holly knew what was different about Jessica, and about this office. It wasn't just a physical brightness in the change of lightbulbs, or pictures of smiling people that made things in this office look different. It was Jessica's new attitude, radiating from her because of her walk with the Lord. It wasn't just displayed in things hanging on the wall, although when Holly looked around, she noticed a wonderful poster with words from the Psalms on the wall in a location where both Jessica and visitors to her office could see it as a reminder of God's goodness.

Holly could feel herself smiling, reminded again about how good God was in every situation. "We sure can. And if you want to, we can pray together right now for that, and a little guidance on how to spend the rest of this Christmas present money from Jake in a way that will make his mom happy, honor the Lord *and* do the best things for the shelter."

Half an hour later Holly was on her way to the office, buoyed up by the prayer time and discussion she'd had with Jessica, and the knowledge that she'd gotten this errand done quickly and so well. She stopped at the coffee shop in the lobby, never doubting for a moment that Jake hadn't made coffee upstairs. He drank plenty when it was made, but didn't bother making a pot just for himself. So she ordered a latte for herself and their largest cup of dark roast for Jake, complete with the three ice cubes he always had them put in the cup to bring the brew to his perfect drinking temperature. Going up the elevator took less time than usual, at what seemed like midmorning for her. When she got to her office, there was only one light on and her computer screen was dark, giving the front office an eerie, almost cavelike look. From his slightly open doorway, she could hear Jake talking to himself, and small metallic noises.

She set her coffee down along with her purse and knocked on his door. "Hey, Jake. You mind company as long as I come bearing coffee?"

"Come on in, Holly, as long as you can stand the mess in here."

She started to say something glib about never minding the condition of his office, but froze a step into the place and forced her mouth closed to keep her shock from showing. "Uh, Jake? I think Barclay's computer exploded." The tower housing of the machine was in pieces and there were bits of the insides of the computer strung out over almost every flat surface in the room.

Jake laughed and took the coffee from her. He took a long drink before he said anything, setting the cup down on a small island of clear space on his desk. "I know. It's not the commonest way to find somebody's passwords, but I'm down to desperate measures. See, you can find the BIOS password by taking apart hardware, and I'm figuring that this will lead me to the other passwords I need to open the files he thought he'd hidden. I found them, just can't open them."

"Okay." The room still looked like the elephant's graveyard of computer parts. Holly trusted her boss to do the right thing in most situations, but this was a new one on her. "There sure looks like there's more than one computer in all this."

"There is. Somewhere along the line someone apparently expected this kind of interference. So when I opened up the tower, there were dummy circuits as well as the real thing. I looked around this morning until I found somebody with a similar unit and borrowed it for a little while to compare the innards."

"This means that somewhere in this building is an agent who has no idea that his computer, which he loaned you, is now totally in pieces."

Jake's grin was a delight. "Well, yeah, but it's Bob. He doesn't use his computer all that much anyway, and I'm nearly to the point of putting it back together. He'll never know what it went through. In fact, it will probably run smoother once he gets it back."

Holly just shook her head. "As long as mine's in one piece. Now give me your lunch order. I've already decided I'm going to run over to the café and bring stuff back about one. From now on we're eating healthy and keeping to as regular hours as possible."

"Yes ma'am," he said, throwing her a mock salute. "And thanks for the coffee. It really hit the spot."

"You're welcome." Holly was surprised he even noticed. If she had this much hardware strung across her office, she wouldn't have noticed a mere cup of coffee. She did the rest of her morning's work to the accompanying tune of Jake putting the two computers back together and continuing to talk to himself while he did it. As far as Holly was concerned, there were few sweeter sounds outside the church choir.

Jake looked around at the piles of stuff in his office, wondering if he could really put it back together as easily as he'd told Holly that he could. She was a great assistant, and thought he could do anything. He hated to disabuse her of that notion. If anything would, it would be this case they were preparing for the prosecutors. Everybody knew that Barclay was working for La Mano Oscura, the drug ring that was bringing tons of junk into Colorado Springs. But Barclay had certainly hidden his connections well. So well that even though he'd ratted out his boss in Venezuela, Baltasar Escalante, there just wasn't the trail leading back to Barclay that would let prosecutors convict him of the worst of the charges against him. They needed proof that matched Escalante's files to Barclay.

While Jake toyed with all the options for opening

those files on Barclay's hard drive that could provide that proof, he put Bob's computer back together. It wasn't a difficult job. During college and in the twelve years since he'd built far more complicated computers himself from parts. In fact, he preferred building his own because it allowed him to look at the circuit boards fairly quickly and see whether or not someone had tampered with anything.

By the time Bob's tower was back together, Holly was at his door again. "Okay, I'm double checking your lunch order before I go over to Aunt Lidia's and get it."

Jake glanced at the watch his long-sleeved shirt hid. "Man, time flies when you're having fun."

"So does the snow. It's been snowing off and on all morning since I came in. Can I borrow your car keys to take Big Red on the lunch run? I'll be nice to him, I promise."

Jake fished around in his pocket. As late as he'd made Holly come in, her Jeep was more than likely in a parking space she'd lose if she left it for lunch now. Especially on a snowy day. Since his spot was reserved, it made more sense to let her drive his vehicle. "Sure. And the soup and sandwich I ordered earlier are fine, unless they have apple pie left this late. Then get me a piece of that, too."

Holly caught the keys he tossed her and grinned. "Already done. I had Aunt Lidia save two slices so they'd be there this late. Otherwise it was no chance. I'll be back in twenty or so."

"See you then." He started putting the screws back into Bob's tower housing, ready to take it back to the other agent. As he'd told Holly, no one would ever know that the machine had been in pieces on his floor and desk half an hour ago.

He'd dropped the unit off in Bob's office and was back, reassembling parts of Barclay's when Holly came in with the bags and bundles that made up lunch. He could hear her rattling around in the outer office, and expected to hear one of her always cheerful greetings. Instead she was standing silently at his doorway a moment later, and she looked upset.

"Hey, you're back. What's up?" He laid down his tools and came to the doorway to greet her. His normally smiling assistant looked on the brink of tears.

"I was careful like always, and I parked in one of the café's twenty-minute spots right in front. I took my eyes off your car only for a minute or two inside." Her lip was trembling.

"It can't be that bad, because you drove back here, right? What happened, did somebody hit Red?" If so, they would have come out the worse for wear unless they were driving the biggest truck or SUV on the market. He couldn't see what Holly was this worked up about.

"Worse. Somebody scratched the paint all the way

down the passenger side. It wasn't a little thing like an accidental door ding, either, Jake. Looked like a screwdriver blade or a key, drawn all the way from front to back." She covered her face with her hands, and Jake thought the usually calm and reserved Holly Vance was going to sob on him. "It's all my fault. I should have just taken my old Jeep. Nobody'd even notice if that happened to it."

"Hey, it isn't your fault. It was probably some thoughtless kid, or somebody with a kid's intelligence anyway, just looking for a little stupid fun. Could have happened anywhere, no matter who was driving."

Holly seemed to calm down a little. "I still feel bad. You drive such nice cars, and keep them up so well. It isn't fair that somebody would do this to one of them."

Jake shrugged. "A whole lot of life isn't fair. Now let's have lunch and afterward I'll go down to the parking garage and take a look. It might not be as bad as you're making it out to be."

Her dubious expression said that it was going to be bad, but Jake still wasn't prepared for the depth of the damage when he stood in the garage half an hour later. The gouge was deep, and ran an easy eight feet across the front fender and both passenger side doors. There was no way this could have been anything but a deliberate, malicious act.

He went back up to the office where Holly was

still cleaning up the remains of their lunch. She hadn't done more than pick at hers, even though Jake had tried to reassure her that this was no big deal. He tried to stay nonchalant even as he asked her questions now.

"Anybody parked next to you on the passenger side when you went in?"

"Nobody. I remember, because there was still snow in the space as if no one had been in it for a while. Even when I came out, there were no fresh tracks over there."

"Did you happen to see any vehicles peel out in a hurry?" Jake was forming a picture in his mind, and it wasn't pretty.

"Hard to tell. In this kind of weather there's always somebody seeing what their truck or SUV will do, the old man against machine thing." Holly had lived here for most of her life, Jake knew. She was familiar with the macho contests that seemed to go on every time it snowed. "I don't know, maybe..."

"Go on. It doesn't hurt to be wrong once in a while."

Her brow wrinkled. "I'm not sure. There might have been a dark-blue SUV pulling out across the street. If I didn't know better, I would have said the driver of that one didn't want me to see him."

"It's something. Not anything I'd bring to the police, or even put on the insurance report I'm going to file, but it's something." It was the kind of something, Jake decided, that made him want to talk to Rose D'Arcy again. And this time he'd tell her that her suspicions that somebody might be out to get him could be on the money after all.

Chapter Three

"I still say this is ridiculous." Jake's expression wasn't quite as grumpy as a frown or a glare, but there was a serious cast to his features that Holly wasn't used to.

She sat at her desk, determined to stick to her guns. "Sorry, this isn't negotiable. I was the one driving when Red got all scarred up. I'll handle all the insurance paperwork. Just give me your card and I'll do it."

"With everything else you have to do?" Jake waved an open hand over her desk, highlighting the piles of paperwork, print requests, sticky-note-covered documents and more that kept them from seeing the surface.

"And your workload, we both know, is going to let you handle this before *next* Christmas?" Holly shook her head. "Face it, Jake, you have to admit I'm right this time. Or at least that my way makes more sense. If you wait until you handle this yourself, it will be February, at least. And if you wait that long, you could be inviting rust spots on Red."

Holly was pretty sure she had him now. While she might not understand what drove her boss to the endless round of social engagements he usually went to, she did know one thing: the two vehicles that he drove were far more important to him than any of the women he went out with. It wasn't a priority she would have chosen in her own life, but it was Jake's.

Jake harrumphed some, and pulled up the side chair next to her desk. Holly felt a twinge of surprise; he never did this unless there was a serious discussion coming on, and she wasn't sure that even repainting one of his precious vehicles rated that.

"Okay, I'll let you do it your way," he said, settling into the chair. "But you have to promise me something."

"What?" Even for Jake, she wasn't about to make promises without hearing the details.

"That you'll be careful while you're out in public with Red. And it's not because I'm afraid for the car, Holly. I'm getting a little bit worried for you."

Now it was her turn to scoff. "What for?"

"It's the case we're working on. When Rose was here a week ago, she warned me that somebody working for Escalante might target me because of what I'm doing. I didn't believe her then, but I'm starting to think she was right. And I don't want my problems spilling over into your life."

Holly blinked. This just hadn't entered her mind before. "Okay, I'll be careful, even though I think you and Rose are probably getting worked up over nothing. You were probably right when you said it was a kid that did this, or just somebody being ignorant."

"I hope it is. But until I can be sure of something like that, I want you to look out for yourself. Human beings are worth more than anything with an engine, Holly, and I want you to remember that."

"I will." It wasn't a sentiment she was prepared to hear from her boss. Especially not said with such warmth and conviction, those blue eyes boring into her in a way that made her feel extremely warm. Suddenly it was time to change the subject to almost anything else.

"So, what's the next step in taking down Alistair Barclay?" The project was taking up more and more of Jake's waking hours, and because of that, her life as well.

Jake shrugged. "You tell me. The man might have been unfamiliar with computers to a large degree, but somebody working for him was very, very good with them. And the programs that someone wrote to hide and encrypt Barclay's personal files are good. I keep thinking there's something I'm missing that could help me unlock all this, but I don't know what it is."

Jake was already looking through his open office door, anxious now to get back to the puzzle. "Go in there and work on it. I'll tell you if I'm going any farther than the copier in the hall, okay?"

"I expect no less." And whatever else she knew, Holly was sure that she'd do whatever Jake Montgomery expected of her. He headed to his office, and she went back to untangling the piles of notes and paperwork on her desk.

As she plowed through the piles of stuff, sifting out the important tasks and taking care of them, setting aside what she could for later, an idea began to form in Holly's mind.

By eleven that morning she'd gotten through the worst of the piles of paperwork on her desk, and made the phone calls and e-mails that were necessary to take care of the things that came next. She knocked on Jake's partially closed door. "I'm going to the drive-though insurance claims office and I have one other stop to make on some errands. So I'll need your car keys. And yes, before you ask, I have my cell phone." She hadn't worked for Jake this long without being able to answer at least half the routine questions before he asked them.

He smiled wanly. "I figured you had your cell phone. And now you're going to ask if I want you to bring back lunch, right?"

"Wrong. I'm going to remind you that you have the monthly update lunch meeting to get all the regional heads-up bulletins. Even I can't get you out of that one. It starts in an hour. If I'm not back, do I need to call you and remind you?"

Jake looked positively glum. "I guess not. Some things I have to remember on my own. Which is a shame, because I'd really love to tell them I forgot this one. Meetings. Bah, humbug."

"Gee, all you need now is a Santa hat and you'd be right into your normal holiday spirit," she teased. Of course it wasn't far off. Jake went to the usual round of society and charity holiday events every year, but he grumbled about wearing a tux and doing the party circuit every time. He might be more than a little relieved to get out of most of that, given the evidence he needed to build against Barclay. Holly felt like telling him the best news of all—that she might have found the key to unlocking the codes he'd been working on for over a week. But in case her idea was out of line, she held off. No sense in giving Jake false hope. She borrowed his keys and went off on her errands, trying to keep from whistling cheery tunes as she left the building.

An hour later she was done with the insurance claim business and cruising down the side streets of Colorado Springs, looking for El Rey Construction. She found it without too much problem, and went into the shabby building, hoping to find the one person who could make her boss's day.

What was up with Holly? Jake wondered about her lighthearted demeanor this morning, even as he worked on Barclay's computer for an hour and then went to the dreaded staff meeting. It was as awful as usual, replete with boring turkey sandwiches and vapid little tree-shaped sugar cookies to remind him of the season he was spending behind his office door.

There wasn't much information in the presentation that he could use right now for anything, but mandatory meetings were just that, so he suffered through as long as he had to, and fled the moment he could for his office.

He was back at Barclay's now reassembled computer, but it still was not yielding all of its secrets. He'd tried every random compiler he knew of, and still wasn't having any luck with the series of passwords that would let him open the files he was sure had the information that would link Barclay with Baltasar Escalante.

While he was still muttering over the last fruitless series of code breakers, Jake heard Holly come into the outer office. She was so incredibly cheerful today, which was a surprise. Yesterday she'd been almost beside herself because the car had gotten scratched while she was driving it. Now today she was humming Christmas carols. It just wasn't like her.

She knocked on his half-open door, and it was all Jake could do not to growl at her. He felt like Ebenezer Scrooge holed up in there, crabbing at Bob Cratchit. Except Scrooge's clerk had never been as good-looking as the young woman who burst through his door, nearly giggling about something. This was the strangest happening of the week. The sedate, staid Holly Vance, almost giggling? Maybe the stress of the long hours was getting to her.

"Okay, what's up? I have never seen you in this kind of mood before," Jake said, getting up out of his chair.

"Blame it all on Miriam Atwater!"

"Who's she? And what did she do to put you in this frame of mind?"

"Miriam is an administrative assistant at El Rey Construction. But that's not the really good part. Do you know what she did for a living before November 15?"

"Not a clue. But you're going to tell me, I'm sure."

"She was Alistair Barclay's personal secretary."

"I don't think so. Wasn't his assistant that drippy little character Rose already deposed...what was his name...Brimble or something?"

"Trimble. Carlton Trimble. And he was Barclay's personal assistant. Merely an honorary position, to hear Miriam tell it, sort of like a valet, only work related. Trimble's some kind of relation to Barclay, third cousin once removed or something on his mother's side. Our Ms. Atwater was the one who did the day-to-day stuff, like I do for you."

Suddenly Jake was beginning to understand Holly's bubbly mood. It was almost catching, in fact. "If she's anywhere near as efficient and helpful as you are, she knows everything there is to know about Barclay."

"I should blush. Thanks for the compliment."

How had he never noticed before the way Holly's deep-brown eyes shone when she was happy? Was this the first time he'd ever seen her this excited about something? If so, he really felt like Scrooge.

"But yeah, she knows a lot. And given the lousy situation she found herself in when Barclay decided to hide her away at El Rey, she was more than happy to have lunch with me and discuss all sorts of things."

"I hope you took her somewhere nice, and put it on my tab." Jake was also thinking he'd need to call Rose this afternoon and tell her of another potential witness to depose in Barclay's case.

"We had the quietest table possible at the Stagecoach. And we even used her car, which I'll have you know came back to El Rey unscathed." She seemed proud of the fact, and Jake almost laughed.

He sat down at the desk again and rebooted Barclay's computer. It only took a moment for him to get the commands through to find the phantom files that wouldn't open. "Okay, so what do you think are the passwords to these babies?" The cursor blinked at him teasingly.

"Let me go get my notebook." Holly dashed back to her office, and came back with a small memo book. "Okay, let's look at the list. Miriam and I had a great lunch. I know more about Barclay than I ever wanted to know, including where he went to have that horrible hair job taken care of weekly. Ick." She actually shuddered. Jake could understand her being repelled by the conversations that must have gone on. She flipped through the notebook and sat down in the chair beside his desk.

"Can you find the creation date on the file you need to open?"

"That much I can do, for what little good it does me. So far I haven't found anything related to the date that suggested a password. Let's see…the first one was August 27."

Holly looked in her notebook. "August. Okay, try *Trixie* for a password."

Trixie? Feeling like an idiot, Jake typed in the name. Wonder of wonders, the file opened. He stifled a whoop. "Oh, this is great. Let's try another one. September 15."

"Bubbles."

This was too good to be true, but it worked. "Unreal. We're on a roll, here. October 10."

"Tiffani. With an *i* on the end, not a *y*."

"November 9." One last one and they had the whole series. Of course, this was all still coded somehow, but at least it was open for him to start decoding.

"Hmm. That one's a little fuzzy. Try Suzette. If that doesn't work, go for…" She looked at the page hard, and then closed her eyes. "Oh, boy. Just try Suzette first and we'll cross our fingers. The other one's too embarrassing to say out loud."

"You're lucky." Suzette worked, opening the last file.

"All right, explain this. How on earth did you find these passwords?"

Holly grinned again. "Like I said, I took Miriam to lunch. We talked a lot about her former boss and all his bad habits, including the fact that he was all over town at every social event possible, and always with a different…uh…flavor of the month, so to speak." Her cheeks took on a shade of rose Jake didn't think possible. First giggling and now blushing? He was seeing more depth to Holly in this one conversation than he'd found out in two years.

"So these are all the names of his…companions of the moment?"

Holly nodded. "For all his canny behavior in some areas, Barclay didn't strike me as too bright in others. And you've said before that somebody more than likely set up his computer system for him, including the encryption. That he wasn't all that computer savvy. So I figured he'd want passwords that were easy to remember for him, but wouldn't make much sense to anybody else unless they knew him well."

Jake shook his head. "What a loser. Not only did he use these girls just to be seen with them out in public, but he reduced them to a list of possibilities for passwords."

Holly shrugged. "You knew he wasn't a nice man, Jake. And it's not likely that he saw these young women as people. From what Miriam said, he doesn't see much of anybody as people, just means to an end. That was what made me think of getting the list of names from her, with her trying to remember which ones came when. Maybe if her boss had been more considerate of them, and of her, Miriam wouldn't have this information to pass on to us."

Now this was the Holly he knew, more thoughtful and quiet. Still, Jake was so excited to have a solution after the hours of work he'd put in that he was almost beside himself. "Well, remind me to appreciate you and be considerate of you, plenty. Holly, you're a genius."

They both stood at once, and the pat on the shoulder he reached out with in congratulation became something else. Jake wasn't sure how their bodies got that close to each other that quickly. All of a sudden the simple pat on the shoulder he'd intended became more of a collision, with Holly stumbling a half step toward him, eyes wide. His reflexes were good, and he grabbed Holly to keep them both from crashing to the floor. That's all it was, a movement to steady them both.

But somehow it turned into something else as their bodies collided and Holly's flushed face got closer and closer to his own, his arms around her in his split-second reaction to their mishap. His arms closed around her instinctively at first, then even more strongly as the warm, supple feel of her registered in his brain.

Her surprised, parted lips were there, and the jolt when they met his nearly knocked Jake off his feet in a way the accidental impact hadn't. It was the briefest of kisses, surely nothing like those he shared with any of the half-dozen casual dates he'd had in the past months. But this was Holly, not some casual date. This was like nothing he'd experienced before and it stunned him.

"Wow. Sorry. I mean…Holly, you're still a genius." He let go of her in a hurry, but they still stood very close together next to his desk. He was so aware of her, from the texture of her soft sweater to the floral scent of her shampoo.

"Thank you. For the compliment." She seemed even more stunned than he did. "Guess the other was…"

"The heat of the moment. Won't happen again."

"No, it won't." Her answering smile was brief, and

somewhat saddened. It reminded him all too much of the Holly he saw every day, and made him wonder what had built the wall around her that she kept so staunchly in place.

"Thank you again for this information, Holly. I can't say enough to tell you how important it is to the case." He looked back at his computer screen, anxious to save all the information he now had access to.

"You're welcome, Jake. And now I'll let you get back to work." She wasn't humming Christmas carols any more, Jake noticed. But it was the last thing he noticed that afternoon about Holly, as the new information she'd handed him enticed him back to his quest for Alistair Barclay's hide.

Holly sat at her desk, trembling. What on earth had just happened? Had she really kissed Jake? Surely not. At the very least, she'd certainly let him kiss her. It just didn't make sense. Her relationship with Jake Montgomery was strictly business. There was no room in it for kisses or anything else of that nature.

Still shivering, she tried to deal with all her confused, tumultuous thoughts. This was the first time in nearly five years that anyone had kissed her. At least anyone male, whom she might have cared about in a romantic sort of way. She hadn't had a date, or a kiss, since the last trial she'd been this involved with had finished up. That one had been much more traumatic and closer to home.

Will it ever be over, truly over and behind me? she wondered, tears in her eyes. She breathed a silent prayer that Jake would stay involved in his work for the time it took to compose herself and get back to work herself. Looking around the office, she tried to find something that would draw her into the task at hand without making her think of the kiss she had shared with Jake.

Miriam Atwater's address and phone number were there directly under her purse, written on a slip of paper that stuck out from under a corner of the leather. Holly pulled out the slip and got out the note cards she kept in her desk for special occasions. Willing her hands not to tremble, she grabbed a pen and began a note to the older woman. "Dear Ms. Atwater," Holly wrote. "Thank you again for our delightful conversation at lunch. I cannot begin to tell you how much Mr. Montgomery appreciated your help." By the time the note was finished, her hands had stopped shaking, and Holly was able to go on about more mundane tasks that kept her busy the rest of the afternoon and into the early evening while Jake stayed in his office.

She expected him to say something about their earlier encounter when she wished him good-night after dark, but he was so engrossed in Barclay's computer that she had to call to him twice just to get his attention. And only the fact that he'd obviously changed shirts and wore a different pair of wool slacks the next morning told her that he'd gone home at all in between her "goodbye" that night and her "hello" the next morning.

"How early did you get in here? Or did you just stash a change of clothes somewhere that I didn't know about?" she asked suspiciously.

"And good morning to you, too," Jake piped up. "Can't you tell that I've been home, had one of my mom's home-cooked dinners and a great night's sleep, and even a nice workout at the club this morning?" His blue eyes sparkled to match the grin he wore.

"Maybe, if I look real hard. Did you honestly go over to your mom's for dinner?" Holly found that part hard to believe. She had been sure that Jake would have stayed late into the evening after finding the key to unlocking Barclay's secrets.

"Well, no, I cheated on that part. When I was over there the last time she handed me a stack of frozen dinners she'd made up for me. She said that now that she doesn't have to worry about how Adam's eating anymore since he's married, she only has me to fuss over. Colleen won't let her."

"Figures," Holly said. "Still, I'm glad you got a hot meal. It makes me feel better about not stopping for bagels or anything this morning." She looked over to the credenza in surprise. "And you even made coffee yourself?"

Jake huffed a bit. "I am capable, you know. I'll admit to having to ask Sara about the filters, but otherwise it came out just fine. I figured that since you'll have plenty to do today, I could get that much done by myself."

"Thanks. Now to get to that pile of sticky notes you've already left for me and start getting everything going." Holly even poured herself a cup of the coffee Jake had made, silently wondering if it would be drinkable. Surprisingly, he could make decent coffee. She thought about telling him that perhaps they should take turns all the time. There was no reason she had to spoil him.

She smiled as she saw the top note on the pile. "Send Miriam Atwater a dozen roses," the note said in her boss's bold hand. It also directed her to tuck a generous gift certificate to the nicest local department store in with the card. So Jake had actually heard what she'd said about Barclay treating his former assistant badly. She hummed a little while she worked through the rest of his directives. Jake was the best boss she could think of possibly working for.

"I feel silly letting you do this," Jake said, trying to sound stern. He knew that Holly's time was less valuable than his right now, especially when he was making such progress on the Barclay files. But she was running so many of his personal errands that whatever life she had otherwise had to have evaporated by now.

"Can't be helped," she said with a shrug, making the Christmas tree pin on her red sweater sparkle. "Besides, I still say that I should be handling all the insurance runaround on your vehicle anyway, since I was the one driving it—"

"You've used that argument enough, Vance. Let's just say I appreciate this, and I owe you one."

She stuck her chin out, looking a little stubborn about letting him cut her off in the middle of her argument. "I still think it's a shame they don't have a loaner to give you for the afternoon while they paint your car. If they did you wouldn't even have to come get me in my Jeep later. You won't forget, will you?"

Jake chuckled. "So that's the real reason you were so unhappy about the loaner not being available. You think I'll get involved in work and forget to pick you up, don't you?"

"It could happen." She looked a little put out at being caught, but Jake could have told her she was right. It could certainly happen, and he'd have to set the alarm on his watch to make sure it didn't.

Only the insistent beeping forty-five minutes later pulled him out of his fog at the computer and made him scramble for his coat and Holly's car keys, looking up the address of the body shop where she had taken the Escalade.

Traffic was heavy for a weekday afternoon, and Jake found himself hunting for a parking place on the side street the auto body shop occupied. Nothing was available in the lot there, and the places closest to the shop along the street were taken as well. He had to drive past the place, honking for Holly, who seemed pulled out of some kind of reverie by the sound. He motioned that he'd turn around and get the one spot available across the street, and she nodded. As he did just that, she craned her neck to find an opening in the traffic herself and cross over to where he was pulling over.

Jake concentrated on parallel parking the unfamiliar vehicle for what seemed like only thirty seconds. Yet as he did so, there was the sound of squealing tires and blaring horns, and he looked up to see Holly fall back toward the curb. Leaving her car still running, the keys in the ignition, he was across the avenue in a flash. "Holly! Are you all right?"

She sat on the curb between two parked vehicles, rubbing one knee and looking dazed. "I'm okay, I think. I guess that guy just didn't see me.... He sure headed for me awfully fast." Jake looked up the street where the taillights of a vehicle that might have been a dark-blue SUV were disappearing rapidly around a corner.

"I'm afraid he saw you just fine," he said, trying not to clench both fists. "Let me go shut off your car. Then come on back inside the shop while I make some phone calls. First I'm calling Rose, and then the police department. Somebody truly is out to take me off this case any way they can." His heart was pounding as if he'd run miles, not just across the street, because Jake Montgomery was having awful thoughts. Someone might be out to unnerve him, but they'd almost harmed Holly instead and that wasn't going to happen as long as he was drawing breath.

Chapter Four

Holly looked at her boss, certain that he had finally sprouted a second head. The man was crazy, and she didn't think she'd ever say that about Jake. Sure, he could get wrapped up in work, but this kind of over-reacting was just not like him. She sat across the table at the Stagecoach Café, where in another example of overreacting, he had insisted that Lidia and Fiona open up just for them, an hour after their normal lunch closing. That was odd enough, but what he'd proposed once they sat down was just out of the question.

"No," she told him, trying to make her voice as firm as possible. "*I* am not leaving the office and going into hiding. *You* are not leaving the office and going into hiding. *Nobody* is going to do such a ridiculous thing."

Jake's blue eyes glowed with a fervor she hadn't seen before, and it made Holly even more rattled than the crazy driver who missed her with his car this afternoon. "I'm not backing down on this one, Holly. You're going somewhere, and I'm going with you until this trial prep is over or we figure out who's targeting me. I won't put you in more danger."

The strength of his words made shivers run up her spine. "I don't really feel like I'm in danger. Surely not enough to turn tail and hide somewhere." She stirred the cup of cappuccino Aunt Lidia had insisted on making her, heavy on milk and cinnamon. It should have been comforting, but right now Holly wasn't sure that anything that came in a cup was capable of calming her down.

Jake's right eyebrow quirked up in challenge. "Let's see…so far we've been followed at least twice between the office and the courthouse, my vehicle's been vandalized while you were driving it, and you were nearly run down in front of me. How much more has to happen before you call it danger?"

When he put it that way, there wasn't much argument. Still, it sounded like overreacting for Jake to want her to leave. "This seems so cowardly somehow," she grumbled. "And it's a definite lack of faith."

Jake's expression hardened even more. "Cowardly? I don't think so. This is sensible, not cowardly.

And faith, the kind of blind faith you're talking about, is where you and I part company, Holly. I know you're willing to trust God to keep you safe, but for me, I haven't seen God patrolling down here with a Beretta."

"That's not the way life works, and you know it, Jake Montgomery."

He shook his head. "I've seen life work just that way too often to put a lot of trust in this faith business. I know you have that kind of faith, and I know my parents do, but you haven't seen what I've seen."

It was on the tip of Holly's tongue to tell him just how much she'd seen. Still, if she told Jake any more about her own past, he'd just be more protective of her right now and that was the last thing she wanted. "I don't think this guy can do anything that the Lord won't protect me or you from, no matter what you believe. And I still feel that hiding out someplace now just shows a lack of faith in God's promises of protection."

Jake's chin jutted out. "Fine, then. Feel that way. But prepare to feel that way somewhere else, because we are definitely going to go to a safe house or another protected location until it's safe to do otherwise."

Holly felt her resolve melting faster than the foam on her cappuccino. "You're not backing down, are you?"

"Not a chance. Too many people have already

shed blood over this case for me to give up now and let Barclay and Escalante think they've won. And that's exactly what it will look like if we let them distract us from putting together the evidence that will convict Barclay in a few short weeks."

Now Holly felt even more defeated. Just moments ago she pictured Jake as her defender, a knight in shining armor protecting her from the world. Now it looked like he was protecting the evidence in the Diablo case, and she was just a side issue.

"So where do we go? My place is out and so is yours," she said.

"That's the truth. If this guy has been tracking us this closely, my loft is the first place he'd look. Besides, it's no place for a lady." If she didn't know better, Holly would have said Jake was blushing. The ruddy cast to his cheeks made him look even more attractive than usual.

"And my mom would never put up with you moving in, even to protect me. I guess this would be less of an issue if I'd gotten an apartment like I'd planned." It was long past time for her to move out on her own again, but Holly had put it off for one reason or another for close to two years now. When she'd moved back to Colorado Springs from Ohio, living in the house she'd grown up in was comforting. She'd needed shelter from her own personal storms, and her mom was still getting used to widowhood after Dad lost his battle with cancer. Now they were both at a point where moving on was probably the right thing to do. Maybe once this case was over, Holly thought, she and her mother could sit down and talk the situation through.

"I doubt that an apartment would solve the problem," Jake said, breaking into her thoughts. "Whoever he is, he's probably got your place staked out, too. It wouldn't be any different whether it was a house or an apartment complex. We need to go someplace more remote and protected. At this point I don't even want to use any of the bureau safe houses if there's another alternative."

"You're giving this guy more credit than he probably deserves." Holly tried to cross her legs under the table, but found the sore spot on her knee where she'd grazed it earlier.

"Maybe so. But I'd rather give him more credit than less and be sorry about it later. Peter couldn't ever pinpoint the mole in Escalante's organization back here in Colorado. For all we know, the guy stalking us could be government, and good at what he does. I've got a call in for Rose to see if she's got any ideas on where to put us."

Now that she had stopped rejecting the idea of hiding out altogether, a thought was beginning to grow in Holly's mind. "What, exactly do we need in this hideout?"

"Safety. A remote location. And enough tech support to let me get all this evidence squared away while you help me." Jake's brow furrowed. "Which is why it's going to be hard to find a safe house that will meet our needs. They're just not built to accommodate heavy-duty computer equipment."

"What would you say if I told you I had the perfect place?"

Jake cocked his head. "One you'd actually agree to go to, that meets our needs?"

"It will if you give me twenty-four hours," Holly told him. Her mind was racing now with all the different things she had to accomplish. Twenty-four hours would be pushing it, and her brother Mike would skin her alive when she told him what she had in mind.

"You've got it, on one condition. You will not, under any circumstances, be alone at any time in those twenty-four hours. Got it?" His piercing blue gaze made her shiver again. Holly wrapped her hands around her cup, but the warmth had faded from it, and she comforted herself with a silent prayer instead, as she should have done to begin with.

"Got it," she answered, trying to keep her voice steady. "Now take me back to the office for a couple hours."

Jake looked dumbstruck. "You're kidding. You don't want to go straight home?"

Holly shook her head. "Not yet. You have work to get done this afternoon, and so do I. And I have a couple phone calls to make to set this all in motion."

"If you say so. You're certainly one tough customer, Holly." There was an appreciative glint in his blue eyes.

She didn't feel all that tough or brave right now, but Holly knew she had planning to do, and felt that the best place to do it was back at the office with Jake in the very next room. "I'm just following your orders," she told him, watching his puzzled look. "You said you didn't want me alone, right?"

"Right," he said, still looking mystified.

"Well, my mother won't get home until nearly six from the paper. I don't want to worry her this afternoon by telling her to come home early. If I do that, getting her to agree to this for a week will be next to impossible."

Jake groaned. "I'd forgotten about that part. Guess I have phone calls to make, too, letting my parents know I'll be out of touch for a week. This is going to be lots of fun this close to Christmas."

"I know. But we'll manage, I guess. At six you can take me home so that I can pack a suitcase and you can do the same. If this is going to be ready in twenty-four hours, I've got a lot of work to do." Holly stood up, ready to leave her cold coffee and get back to work on this new plan.

* * *

Holly had never seen her mother look quite as surprised as she did that night when she opened the door to find her daughter standing outside with Jake Montgomery beside her. Marilyn Vance was rarely at a loss for words, but she seemed to be as she invited Jake in and offered to put on a pot of coffee.

"Make it tea, Mom," Holly told her. "I've had enough coffee to last me a while, and I suspect Jake's feeling the same way. You've met my boss, Jake Montgomery before, I know."

Marilyn sniffed. "Not only met him, but taught him English, what he learned through high school. I trust you've improved your grammar since then, Jake."

"I've made every effort, Mrs. Vance. But we have more important things to discuss than my past right now. I wanted to explain to you why I'm borrowing your daughter for a few days or more."

"Borrowing my daughter? You know I'm going to start quoting Shakespeare at you if you use that phrase," her mother said, drawing herself up to her full height of sixty-three inches.

"I know, Mrs. Vance. *Hamlet*, Polonius speaking to his son, 'Neither a borrower nor a lender be' and all that, but this time I'm afraid that advice won't work. Holly might be in danger and it's my doing. So until this blows over, we need to go away for a while."

"Just what kind of danger are we talking about, Mr. Montgomery? And where do you intend to take my daughter?" Watching this exchange, Holly wondered if Jake had ever been grilled by someone in law enforcement quite as effectively as her mother was capable of doing.

"I can only answer one of those questions, Mrs. Vance, the one about the danger. Why don't we sit down someplace and I'll explain as much of this as I can to you?"

"You certainly will," her mother said, still sounding as suspicious as she would have been of one of her students handing in a forged permission slip. "Just let me get that tea started. You two make yourself comfortable in the living room. When I come back you can explain why it is you can't tell me where you're going, Jake."

Holly showed him into the living room, aware as she looked around the room that it was probably smaller than the entry foyer of his parents' home. Her family had never done much entertaining or decorating, so the compact room was filled with antique chairs that needed their faded silk upholstery replaced and glass-fronted bookcases that still held her father's old medical books as well as her mother's leather-bound classics.

In one corner was the tall, skinny fir her mother had insisted they bring home last weekend and decorate with her heirloom glass ornaments. It was strung with popcorn and cranberry garland and there was a battered old wooden Nativity scene under the tree. Holly could distinctly remember the year that her twin brother Kenneth had snapped the head off one of the Wise Men's camels playing airplane with it, getting himself in deep trouble with their mother while their more indulgent father laughed.

She looked at Jake to see what his impression of this homey, somewhat shabby room was. His expression surprised her. "Jake, are you sweating? You look uncomfortable. Why don't you sit down?" Holly pointed toward the most comfortable of the chairs.

"Thanks, I think I will." Jake was definitely a bit pale and looked like he'd been perspiring around the temples.

"What's the matter? Did the day finally get to you?" Jake had been the solid one all day when Holly had felt shaky. True, he'd overreacted as far as she was concerned, but he'd done it with such conviction and strength that he'd finally won her over. Now he sat in her mother's living room looking unwell.

His answering laugh was weak. "No, I'm handling the day okay. If you want to know the truth, it's facing your mother that has me rattled."

Holly felt like giggling. Her mother? Marilyn might have been a tyrant in the classroom, but that was over fifteen years ago for Jake. "I don't think she's going to bring up your sophomore English grades, Jake," she said softly, trying to stifle the laughter she felt.

"Probably not." His blue eyes widened. "But I'll tell you the truth, Holly. I'd rather face a dozen guys like that maniac who tried to mow you down today than take on your mother. With my own mom, and even my aunts, I could always charm my way out of anything. Your mother never bought it. And now I've got to sit in her living room and explain to her why I'm spiriting you away for probably a week or more."

"It will be okay. Once I tell her where we're going she'll be all right with it."

He smiled a little. "Does that mean you're going to tell me our destination?"

Holly shook her head. "Nope. You told me to keep it as much a secret as possible. I figured that meant from you as well."

His grin was wider now. Jake leaned forward and chucked one index finger under her chin. The mildest of his touches made her shiver. His voice was husky as he spoke. "You're tougher than I thought you were, Holly. Maybe you should think about going for a position in the bureau higher up than just support staff."

Holly's mother came into the room with a teapot and cups on a tray just in time to hear that remark. Jake moved his hand before Marilyn saw the gesture.

"Don't you dare encourage her in anything like that, Jake. It's bad enough she works down there with all those guns and felons. I'd worry constantly if she were an FBI agent."

Holly moved a small table in front of the settee so her mother could put down the tray. "You don't have to worry, Mom. Jake couldn't convince me to do what he does. And you shouldn't be concerned about me. I'm probably safer at work most days than you are, in the lobby of the newspaper building."

Marilyn lifted the teapot and poured Jake a cup. "You might be right there. Those older gentlemen who come in to complain about where the carrier left their papers do get fairly irate. And they never seem to appreciate it if I point out that the carrier doesn't *lie* the newspaper on the porch anyway, he *lays* it there, or *places* it there." Her expression was pensive. Holly didn't dare look over at Jake for fear of them both exploding into laughter. It would be good for Jake, but it would miff her mother, and that was the last thing they needed right now.

An hour later Jake had driven her Jeep to his loft and Holly was in the kitchen helping her mother clean up the tea things. "Are you sure that this will be all right?" Marilyn asked with more concern than Holly was used to seeing her mother exhibit. "I haven't had to worry about you in a while."

"Since I came back to Colorado, you mean," Holly said softly, drying the antique teapot with infinite care.

"No, it was a while after you came back that I stopped worrying. Once you talked to that counselor at the Galilee shelter, and kept going to church regularly. And you started eating regularly again and stopped having the nightmares."

Holly winced. "I didn't know you knew about the nightmares."

"It was hard not to hear them. That and the fact that you spent a lot of nights sleeping on the couch with the lights on and the television going. For a while I was afraid that man had won."

"He never won, Mom," Holly told her, taking a thin-shelled porcelain cup from her. "I wouldn't let him. God wouldn't let him. Victor Convy might have possessed my body for a very short time, but he never had my soul or my mind or my heart. I gave those to Jesus a long time ago, and nobody as awful as Victor Convy will ever change that."

Marilyn kept washing the dishes, occasionally looking out the kitchen window into the midwinter darkness. Holly was glad that her mother's sharp, dark gaze wasn't fixed on her, didn't see her hands tremble while she dried the dishes. Her words were brave and she tried to convince herself that she meant every one of them. This new threat had shaken her resolve a little.

"You don't think that what Jake was talking about could be connected with that man, do you?" No matter how many times Holly said the name of the man who had attacked her five years ago, her mother would not speak it out loud.

"No, I don't. You know the Ohio authorities have to notify me if there's even the chance that he ever gets out of jail. This is exactly what Jake said it was…threats aimed at him to keep him from testifying against Alistair Barclay. The drug cartel has plenty of money and way too many connections to the seamier side of life. It would be easy for them to pay somebody off to threaten Jake."

"I'm just sorry you're involved in it. You wouldn't consider quitting, would you? Or even just going on some sort of leave?" Marilyn's voice was hopeful.

"It wouldn't help. If I left now, the syndicate would have just what they needed. Nobody else could back up Jake well enough on this short notice. The trial is going to go on no matter what. For it to go on with Jake's best testimony, I have to help him."

"If you say so." Her mother's voice held a note of doubt. "At least I know where you'll be. How did you ever get Michael to agree to this?"

Holly grinned, glad that her mother still gazed out the window and couldn't see her expression. "Let's just say I called in a whole bunch of favors. And he's a good brother."

"He certainly is. With this all happening, I think I'll take him up on his offer to spend Christmas at the ranch. He always says we should, and I always drag him into town instead. Now if we could just convince Kenneth to take leave as well…"

"You're pushing for a miracle there, Mom. But that's okay. You can always try for one." Holly looked out into the cloudy darkness herself, questioning how many miracles one family could actually expect even in this season of wonders. If nothing else, attempting to get Kenneth home on leave from the air force would keep her mother's mind occupied and that was nothing short of miraculous in itself.

She whispered a quiet prayer of thanks as she put the teacups away. They were so delicate and fragile looking, but they'd been in the D'Arcy family for at least a hundred years. Holly knew porcelain got its strength by going through fire. Maybe this was another one of those times when she was being transformed by God, from plain clay to porcelain by the fires of life. She'd just have to hold on and pray that she could withstand the fire like these beautiful, translucent cups.

In the midst of her thoughts the doorbell rang and Holly put down the last cup gently so that she could race to the door. "All right, I'm here," her older brother Michael said. "How about we get this show on the road?"

Holly hugged him, drawing him into the house. "You're letting all the cold air in. Mom will have a fit. Come in for a couple minutes and say hello anyway. By the time you bring me back tomorrow she'll be at work."

"I guess. You didn't tell her—"

"Of course not," she cut him off. "That was part of the bargain. Now go say hi and bye and I'll grab a toothbrush and jeans and be down here in five minutes."

Michael rolled expressive black eyes. "You've never done anything in five minutes in your life. But then again, Mom will take longer than that to say hello. Scoot so we can get out of here in less than half an hour."

Michael headed back toward the kitchen and Holly scooted upstairs to get herself ready to go. In minutes she'd changed into jeans, boots, a turtleneck and sweater and had tossed what little else she needed into a small overnight bag. By the time she joined her mother and brother in the kitchen, Michael was being tempted with her mother's lacy praline wafer Christmas cookies.

She lifted one off the plate for herself and kissed her mother goodbye. "And you said I was going to hold you up."

Michael smiled sheepishly. "Yeah, well, you know I can't resist these." He looked at their mother. "I'll bring her back in the morning. Want me to stop by the newspaper office and say hello?"

"No, you have plenty to do out there. I hope your sister appreciates what you're doing for her by driving out here tonight and back, and then doing this again tomorrow. Not to mention loaning her the cabin for a week or more."

"Oh, I appreciate it, Mom. Michael really knows how much I appreciate it," Holly said, popping the cookie in her mouth with a flourish. Behind her mother's back she looked at her brother cross-eyed and he returned the favor with a grimace.

When they were settled in his truck a few minutes later and headed out to Highway 24 on the trip to Cripple Creek, Michael finally breathed a sigh that sounded like relief. "Okay, hand them over," he demanded.

"They're in the overnight bag. I can't get to it without taking off my seat belt and I'm not about to do that with you driving. But rest assured, dear brother, that when we get to the ranch I'll give you your precious envelope."

Michael shook his head. "I still can't believe you kept those things all this time."

"Hey, a girl with two rowdy brothers needs insurance." Holly watched the miles go by on the dark roads, smiling to herself. Even after fourteen years Michael hadn't guessed that she would never really have turned over the copies of his teenaged speeding tickets she'd gotten by beating him to the mailbox before their parents got home. Maybe a couple weeks from now when Christmas had come and gone she'd give him a special present by telling him just that. But for now it was fun for him to think he wasn't just being a protective, gruff older brother by hiding her out on his ranch. Tonight it could feel like a trade. Stars broke through the clouds as the truck headed west on the silvery highway and Holly listened to the wheels spin, feeling safe under her big brother's protective gaze.

Chapter Five

"This feels like an FBI setup," Holly grumbled as she walked through the parking garage, trying to call as little attention to herself as possible while pulling a suitcase on wheels and toting a backpack full of toiletries.

"Good. It's supposed to," Rose D'Arcy answered. "It's been carefully planned to keep you two safe. And I don't see anybody who looks like they're watching us, so we're good to go." She led Holly to a sleek black car and opened the trunk. "Put your suitcases in and let's head to the courthouse."

All in all, Holly thought this was probably too much effort to expend on their stalker, but everyone else felt differently, so she'd gone along with their elaborate plan. Her cousin Sam Vance, a detective with the Colorado Springs Police Department, had arrived half an hour before and whisked Jake and his computer equipment away in an unmarked police car. If all had gone well, Jake was waiting for them at the courthouse in the parking garage there, where her Jeep had been parked today to keep it away from the stalker.

She had to admit that it was good not to worry about who might be following them. "So, do you think we're in the clear, Rose?"

"So far." Listening to her cousin, Holly had to roll her eyes. Rose talked like a lawyer, all right, never one to give out any more information than she had to. Of course if that was true, her cousin had been in training for her law degree from childhood. She'd always been the tight-lipped older cousin.

"Don't you think Jake's overreacting about all this? I mean, surely this guy will give up now."

"I wouldn't bet on it. Remember, the Diablo crime syndicate has already killed more than one person to damage this case. And there have been attempts on the lives of several of the principal investigators or their friends and families. You can't be too careful."

Now Holly gave a shiver in her seat. She hadn't thought about things quite this way before. Maybe she should be more grateful to Jake for suggesting that they hide out for a while, instead of feeling put upon for having to set this all up.

"Thanks, Rose. I feel about two inches high now for being resentful of all this," Holly said quietly.

"No, you're just used to taking care of yourself. This is one of those times when you need a little help. I'm glad to be part of it." Rose gave her a quick look before pulling into the courthouse parking garage. "Looks like we got here without any followers. Now let's go find the guys so that you two can be on your way."

In moments Holly was standing by her own Jeep, which had already been loaded with Jake's suitcases and computer hardware. Naturally, there was more hardware than luggage. Jake looked different, having dressed down more than he normally did for the office once Holly told him they'd be roughing it a little on their trip. He looked good in jeans and a nubby cable sweater. She'd chosen a flannel shirt and jeans with an old barn coat herself, but then she had the advantage of knowing where they were going.

Jake insisted on stowing her suitcases while Holly said goodbye to Rose. "You've got our cell numbers, right?"

"And you have mine, I trust. Everything's set up with the country sheriff in…uh…where you're going," Rose looked over at Jake and corrected herself when Holly made a face. "I'd forgotten Jake was in the dark about the location," she said in a near whisper.

"Not that he hasn't tried everything to weasel the information out of me. I'm not sure whether he's testing me to see if I can be trusted with secrets, or if he's that anxious."

"Probably a little of both. I'll look in on Aunt Marilyn for you a couple times, okay?" Rose reached over for a quick hug. "Now go while you still have daylight for the trip."

Holly didn't need much more urging than that to be on the road. She was still feeling skittish about this whole trip, hoping that nobody was following them.

"Do you want me to drive?" Jake asked, grinning.

"Not a chance. For that I'd have to tell you where we're going. You'll know when we get there."

"And not a moment sooner," Jake said with a sigh. "I've said it before, but I still mean it, Holly. You are one tough customer."

Holly was getting the feeling that this was a new quality in women for Jake. Surely the last word that would have described most of his society dates was *tough*. No, they were mostly rich, spoiled, pampered and delicate. Some of them must have some purpose and drive, but she certainly hadn't picked up on either of those qualities from her brief meetings, or from pictures of the women in the society pages.

Jake scanned the rearview mirrors while he and Holly made their way out of town. Holly found herself glancing at him almost as often as she looked at the dials on the dashboard. "So, did we give them the slip?" she asked, trying to sound like one of those old detective movies.

"I think so, sweetheart," he answered, giving her back a fairly decent Humphrey Bogart imitation. "Looks like it's just you and me, kid." The hand he put on her shoulder for a moment as he said it made her shiver in the nicest way possible.

Jake could feel himself relaxing a little as they got farther outside the Colorado Springs city limits. No one appeared to be following them, and they were headed in the direction he had hoped they would be. He knew Holly's brother owned a ranch out near the town of Cripple Creek, and it would make a great place to stay away from their stalker for the time it took to finish building the case against Barclay.

Of course he wondered if the resources he needed would be available in the middle of a cattle ranch, but given that Holly set this up, he wasn't really worried. She was so incredibly efficient that he didn't know what he'd do without her. He glanced over at her, driving the Jeep down the highway in the growing dusk. He couldn't think of too many other women with whom he would have been comfortable riding. Perhaps that was a comment on his overconfident view of his own driving skills.

Her efficiency was the first thing that had attracted him to Holly as an assistant, but these days it was not the only thing he found attractive about her, and he was beginning to look at her as much more than just his right-hand woman at work. She was as strong, confident and stubborn as anyone. And to add to that, she was incredibly attractive physically. Why had it taken two years for him to notice that? Jake wondered. When had he started comparing her to women like Zoe whom he normally dated? And the even bigger question, when had Zoe and her companions started coming in a distant second?

Holly looked even better out of the office than she looked in her everyday business attire, Jake decided. The blue-and-green flannel shirt she wore looked soft and complemented her glossy dark hair. Out here she didn't bother with restraining the masses of waves nearly as tightly as she did in the office; one clip pulled back her long hair in a soft ponytail instead of the more severe French braid that she usually wore. Jake found himself wondering if she ever relaxed enough to let her hair loose. What would it look like framing her face? The thought stirred him in ways that he hadn't thought possible when considering Holly until just a few days ago.

Watching her drive along the highway, Jake decided he needed a lot more sleep than he was getting. Sleep, a good solid meal and maybe even a vacation. What else besides stress could make him think this way about Holly Vance? It wasn't as if she would have anything to do with him as anything but her boss anyway. Sure, she was always there and ready to help him with any project, but she made it clear where she drew the line. Besides, there was no way to describe Holly without mentioning her faith. It shone through in every aspect of her life and he'd seen it. That wasn't for him, Jake was sure. Maybe it was okay for the rest of his family, but not where he was concerned.

He must have been more caught up in his thoughts of Holly than he realized, because her sudden braking of the Jeep surprised him no end. "Dear," she exclaimed, making him wonder if she could somehow read his thoughts. Maybe that was why she was so efficient. She really could anticipate what he needed.

Jake started to say something, then noticed that Holly was pointing at the side of the road. With a shake of his head he cleared out the cobwebs, thanking his lucky stars that he hadn't spoken. Holly hadn't called him a pet name. She was pointing out the good-size doe that had almost bounded onto the roadway, causing an accident. "Good thing we missed it," Jake said, settling back down in his seat. *And it's a good thing I didn't make a colossal fool of myself,* he mentally added.

"I'll say. Can you really see near misses like that every day, Jake, and not believe in the protection of the Lord?"

There was another one of those things that made him sure that Holly would never be the right woman for him, no matter how attractive she was. Not only did she have a depth of faith that he was positive he could never find, but she was so open in talking about it all. The thought of being that sure of something you couldn't see or touch or feel mystified Jake.

Holly was still waiting for an answer. "I sure can. Because for everything like that I've seen, there have been a couple more that happened the other way." Holly seemed to be about ready to argue with him, but she pressed her attractive lips together in a straight line instead and stayed silent. Jake was even more thankful for that than he'd been when they missed the deer. He wasn't ready to argue with Holly again about anything.

The next twenty minutes or so were spent in relative silence in the car. Holly didn't seem inclined to push the point she'd been making, and Jake certainly wasn't going to spark any discussion. So they rode along the quiet roads while he scanned the area behind them in the mirrors. Nothing following them that he could see. He knew from the discussions he'd overheard that Holly and Rose had set up a network of protection with the local authorities. Sam Vance had also assured him that where they were going, they'd be looked after.

It was a comfort to pull up to the gates of the Double V Ranch and know that his speculations on their destination had been right. The place was pretty isolated, and looked solid. Mike Vance had been just enough younger than Jake that he hadn't known him in the years they'd both gone to school in Colorado Springs. He'd been closer to Jake's cousin Quinn's age, and though the two of them hadn't ever been best friends or anything, Jake knew that Quinn didn't have a bad word to say about Holly's older brother. In true Bureau fashion, when it looked like they might be staying with Mike Vance, Jake had checked him out.

Mike came up looking like a solid, serious guy, a good businessman and rancher. Just like anybody else with a three-hundred-acre spread—small for today's market—he was struggling to make a living. But he seemed to be determined to do it. And family appeared as important to him as it did to Jake. If the Vance family was anything like his own, Jake knew that anybody who messed with the baby sister was in for a very hard time.

"Let me get out and handle the gate," Jake said, hand already on the door latch.

Holly nodded. "Go ahead." Jake managed the gate and she drove through, stopping the Jeep on the other side while he made sure the gate was closed tight behind them. He was sure there were probably several other gates between the outside world and any stock that Mike ran on the place, but even as a city boy he knew how ranchers felt about folks who left gates wide-open. No sense offending his host straight off.

"We'll go to the main house and let Mike know we're here," Holly said once Jake settled himself back in the passenger seat. "Then we'll head out to the cabin."

"Cabin?" This was a new one on him. Jake had just assumed that if they were staying at the Double V, they'd be staying in the main house with Holly's brother. He was single, and it was a good-size ranch house.

"Cabin. It's small, out on the ridge away from the main house. I expect back in the old days it was a line shack, but it's gone through at least a couple renovations since then. I can't promise all the comforts of home, but we'll get by."

"I hope so. Does this cabin have running water? Electricity?"

"Plenty of both. You don't think I'd drag you out here in the middle of nowhere without the things you need to convict Barclay, do you, Jake?" Holly's voice was soft, but he could hear a note of irritation in it.

"Not really. You've never let me down yet. It's just hard to imagine a twenty-first-century cabin, I guess."

"Mike's worked on it some from time to time, and when you were talking about getting away yesterday, I called him. Between what he'd already done and what I could swing in a little over a day, it will serve our needs." Holly sounded pleased with herself now.

They were pulling up to the main house, where the circular gravel drive in front held a battered but still serviceable pickup truck and two cars. On the front door was a large evergreen wreath, and there were lights in the windows that made the place look rustic but welcoming.

"Nice place. It looks like a picture postcard just waiting for the Christmas snow," Jake said, meaning every word of it.

"Yeah, well you better hope we don't get any of that snow if you want to get back to Colorado Springs whenever you want for the trial. This is a working ranch, and nobody's going to take time to plow a road for the city folks to get back home." Holly knocked on the front door, not waiting for Jake's reply.

Jake hadn't thought about the animal occupants of the house, and what kind of ruckus might be raised by knocking on the door. Judging from the barking going on, the Double V had a dog pack. He tried not to step away from the door, hoping the beasts weren't as ferocious as they sounded.

The man who opened the door was tall and dark, looking a little older than the thirty-one Jake knew him to be. The skin around his dark eyes was crinkled from sun and wind, and his face creased in a smile when he saw Holly. "Hey, you two finally made it. Come on in."

Before anybody could walk in, two large furry bodies streaked out, and Jake steeled himself for all the possibilities. What he wasn't expecting was that the largest dog would bound up to Holly and ignore him completely. "Hi, King. How's my buddy? Did you miss me?"

"You've only been gone about twelve hours and he's *my* dog, Holly," her brother pointed out. Looking down at the beast, he grimaced. "But yeah, you can tell he missed you."

"King only pretends to be Mike's dog because he lives here. He'd be mine in a heartbeat if I stayed out here for more than a day at a time."

"I'd argue with her, but she's right," Mike said, stepping around the dog and his sister to Jake. "Molly, the Australian shepherd over there, now she's all mine. But it looks like she'd make friends with you if you gave her half a chance."

Mike had a firm handshake when Holly introduced him, and he looked Jake straight in the eye. "You've done plenty to make my life miserable in the last two days. I certainly hope you're worth it."

Jake, not used to seeing much emotion out of Holly, wasn't prepared for the shriek she gave, or the mostly playful way she launched herself at her brother. If the dog was upset at her berating his master, he sure didn't show it. Even Molly stayed closer to Jake, interested now in the hand he'd put out in greeting. "Mike, what are you doing? This is my *boss!* Do you want me to come out here and sponge off you because I'm unemployed? Knock it off."

"Sure. But you have to admit that this has been a pain, Holly. I haven't gotten anything worthwhile done since yesterday noon between waiting for the guys you called to do stuff to the cabin, and driving you around...." He sounded every bit as put upon as Jake knew he would have been if Colleen had asked a big favor of him. And Mike had the same indulgent, loving expression on his face Jake would have worn in a similar situation.

"And you'll thank me for it later, I know."

"I expect Holly to have charged out anything major to the Bureau," Jake said. "I know some of this stuff isn't anything you'd have done on your own, and we couldn't use any of the local safe houses for the high-tech stuff we're doing."

"We'll talk about that later. Right now I'm having too good a time using it as leverage on my sister," Mike said with a grin. "Come on in and have a cup of coffee and some of Dorothy's Christmas cookies. Bringing cookies back from Mom's yesterday put my housekeeper in a competitive mood, and you can't leave me here with a kitchen full of goodies."

He motioned toward the back of the house and visitors and dogs all followed him into a large, well-lit ranch kitchen where a woman in her fifties was taking cookies off a baking sheet and laying them out on racks on a long heart-pine table. The room smelled of cinnamon and sugar and was filled with warmth from the oven. King and Molly headed to a couple of round plaid beds in the corner, settling in with contented canine sighs.

Jake took a deep breath in the fragrant room. He knew that the long hours of the trial prep had knocked a couple pounds off of him, but he suspected that a few days at the ranch faced with Dorothy's cooking and he could stop worrying about his suits hanging on him for the trial. In this cozy kitchen it was hard to remember that they were here to keep from losing their lives over a tense legal battle. He'd give them half an hour, Jake decided, to socialize and enjoy this oasis. Then they had to head to the cabin and start work on nailing Barclay again.

Holly could tell that Jake was anxious to get out to the cabin and get settled, but neither Mike nor Dorothy was cooperating with his timetable. First they had coffee and cookies, and then Dorothy realized that the visitors hadn't stopped anywhere for dinner on the way to the ranch.

"And here I went, spoiling your dinner with Christmas cookies," she said, looking positively sheepish. "I didn't even think that at nearly eight at night you hadn't had dinner."

"Don't worry about it, Dorothy," Holly told her, watching Jake's bemused expression. "We had a big lunch, and ate later than usual. When Aunt Lidia found out we wouldn't be stopping by the Stagecoach again before Christmas, she insisted on sending over lunch. There was enough for at least four people."

"She doesn't know where you were going, does she?" Mike's eyes narrowed.

"Definitely not. I just told her we were going to be too busy with trial prep to get out of the office again. Officially, that's the story for everybody except Mom, Rose and Sam."

"What about *your* family, Jake? Do they know how to get hold of you in an emergency?" Holly watched her brother grilling Jake just like he used to grill her dates in high school. She doubted that Jake would be as intimidated. If anybody intimidated him on the ranch, it appeared to be King, who had come and planted himself next to her at the table, watching everyone intently while they talked.

"My family's taken care of. I used the same system I normally use when I'm out of town on Bureau business."

Dorothy was still poking around the kitchen, unable to sit down and sip her cup of coffee with everyone else. "I imagine it's something terribly complicated and technical, with your work in computers. Do you use secret code?"

Jake's laugh was open and honest. "Not exactly. I usually write down a phone number and an address if need be on a slip of paper, seal it in a plain white envelope and give it to my dad. That way he has a contact in a real emergency, and if he doesn't have any reason to use it, he gives me back the envelope unopened when I come back into town."

Dorothy looked deflated. "And here I thought it was going to be something exciting."

"Sorry to disappoint you, Mrs. Miller," Jake told her. "Where my family is concerned, I'm not much for excitement. It's nice to give my folks enough information so that my mother doesn't worry about my job, even though the most dangerous thing I usually do on my out-of-town trips is deconstruct somebody's hard drive."

Holly watched him sit at the big pine table and marveled once again that there were so many sides to Jake. There was the suave, brilliant computer expert that everyone saw at work when he came out of his office long enough to actually be seen. Then there was this Jake, who didn't show up in the limelight much, but just might be her favorite side to his complex personality. Definitely the plainspoken family man with his long, slender fingers wrapped around a steaming china mug of coffee outshone the guy she had seen at parties with his accessory blond and a champagne flute full of ginger ale. If she were only sure that this was the real Jake, she could fall in love with the man.

Holly's thoughts almost made her gasp out loud. Fall in love with Jake Montgomery? No matter how perfect he seemed at any time, that just wasn't an option. And it certainly wasn't the kind of thoughts she should be entertaining when they were getting ready to spend days together in that cabin up on the ridge. She got up from the table so quickly the others focused on her in unison.

"Is something wrong, dear?" Dorothy asked.

"No, just looking at the time," Holly said, trying not to stammer. "We really need to be heading out if we're going to get anything done tonight."

"Let me pack you some sandwiches then, and a few more of those cookies. And make Mike give you at least two more blankets from the closet. That cabin will be cold tonight."

With Dorothy's instructions, everyone was up and moving. Holly looked over at Jake as he brought his coffee cup to the sink along with his empty cookie plate. He had the strangest look on his face, almost as if he'd heard her thoughts about falling in love with him. Holly knew she was beginning to blush up to the roots of her hair.

Things got even more uncomfortable when they had their coats on again and were headed out to the Jeep. King insisted on going along, and even nudged

Jake out of the way when he opened the passenger door, the big Shepherd poised to take his normal place next to Holly.

"No, I don't think so," she told the dog, who looked up at her, plumed tail thumping the ground. "You have to stay here with Mike."

"I don't mind," Jake said, but his tone was hard to decipher. He hadn't looked comfortable around the dogs in the house; if she didn't know better, Holly would have said this was something her normally fearless boss didn't deal with well.

"Are you sure?" Holly asked. The dog gave a soft whine, looking between the two of them. "We can always send him back in the morning if things don't work out."

"That might be for the best. Until then, well, Dorothy said it was cold in the cabin, and as long as he sleeps on your bed I can take an extra blanket," he said with a grin.

Her bed? Holly did a mental inventory of the cabin, realizing one thing for the first time. She'd been so focused on making sure Jake had electricity for the computer, and enough light to work with, and all of the technical details taken care of that she'd neglected the more human side of the arrangements. There was one bedroom in the cabin, with one bed. Suddenly her indecision evaporated. "Hop in, King," she told the dog, who gave a joyful little bark and bounded in between the front seats. She was going to need all the company she could get when Jake saw the close quarters they'd be sharing for the next few days.

Chapter Six

"I don't think that dog likes me," Jake said, looking down at King, who sat by Holly's feet in the main room of the cabin. It was really the *only* room in the cabin, when you got down to basics. True, it was a good-size room, but it was the only one besides the single bedroom that took up half the second story, perched like a loft above the living room. That and the tiny bathroom made up the whole cabin.

At least there was plenty of running water, and a generator or something, because the light switches were there and worked when you threw them. A large, rustic desk in one corner near the flagstone fireplace proved the perfect place for the computer, which hummed to life as soon as Jake set it up. There was a good chair at the desk, easing any tension in his back from the ride out to Cripple Creek, and the slightly battered leather couch Holly sat on with King at her feet looked very comfortable. The dog, however, still watched Jake intently. He wasn't growling, but he didn't appear to be man's best friend, either.

Holly leaned back on the couch, still burrowing her fingers into the dog's fur between his ears. "Nonsense, Jake. King's my buddy. He likes you just because I do, right, boy?" The dog's tail thumped as Holly spoke to him, but Jake still wasn't sure about the look the big beast gave him.

"What are you going to do with him at bedtime? For that matter, what are you going to do with *me* at bedtime? I took the grand tour of the place, and there's only one bed in that bedroom. Being the gentleman that I am, I have to insist you take the bed."

"You're too kind. And normally I'd take you up on it, but when I'm at the ranch, King usually insists on sleeping next to me."

Smart dog, Jake thought, watching the big animal lean back into Holly's caresses. "So why does that mean you won't take the bed?"

Holly looked at him as if he'd lost his mind. Maybe there was something about the whole situation he was missing. "Dogs don't climb ladders. Or open-backed steep stairs that look like ladders. He'd get up there okay, I imagine, but he'd never get down. And he's way too big to carry, even for you."

She had him there. Just the thought of hauling

eighty pounds of dog down a ladder didn't do a thing for him. Especially this dog, who kept looking at him as if he were prime rib. "So I either act like a hound and take the bed away from a lady, or make friends with a hound and let you sleep up there alone?" He gave her a smile he hoped was charming.

For some reason, his charm never worked on Holly. Maybe that was part of why he was beginning to find her so enticing. She did smile back at him, anyway.

"That about sums it up. For tonight you take the bed. You have to be as tired as I am, or worse. Tomorrow morning maybe we'll go back to the main house for breakfast, and I'll convince King to stay over there with Mike. He'll get bored just following me around the cabin here anyway, won't you, guy?" The plumed tail thumped again, and Jake couldn't help envying all the attention the dog was getting. Holly didn't talk that way to him.

"I guess that's all right," he said, still not overly thrilled with an arrangement that let him have what looked like a perfectly good bed while Holly shared the sofa bed with a dog. "You'll be warmer down here in front of the fire, anyway."

"And ready to go to sleep before long. Don't think you'll keep me up if you work on the computer, because I'm tired enough that you won't. But don't stay up all night working on that, either. Get some rest yourself and start fresh in the morning."

"I will," Jake told her, not sure even as he said it if he should promise that. If he had enough luck tracing Barclay's coded entries, he could be in front of the screen for hours. Even now it was beginning to pull him in. Before he knew it, Holly had gone up the bedroom stairs and started doing things to get ready for bed. King planted himself at the base of the stairs, occasionally whining softly.

When she came down, she spent a little time in the small bathroom with the door shut, causing the dog to complain a little more. Then she came over to the couch in a velour sweatsuit and fuzzy socks, carrying a pillow and blanket. "Good night, Jake. See you in the morning."

"Good night," he said, barely looking up from the computer screen, where Barclay's code had already drawn him in again. A few minutes later he pulled himself out of his reverie, expecting to see her already asleep. Her breathing had softened to a slow rhythm. When he looked over, Jake could see her nestled under the blanket, one hand still on King's head.

Her hair was spread out in a halo over the pillow, and Jake thought that it was every bit as enticing as he'd imagined. With a start he realized that even though her eyes were closed, Holly didn't seem to be asleep, unless she talked to herself in her sleep. After a moment, he looked away, feeling a little embarrassed. She was praying, he realized. Leaving her all the privacy he could in the close quarters of the cabin, Jake went back to his work.

When Holly woke with light streaming in the cabin windows, she almost expected to see and hear Jake at the computer. Even though he'd said he would turn in early, the two times that she'd stirred from sleep to put another log on the fire, he was still at the computer. "Come on, Jake, give it a rest," she muttered the second time.

"I will. Soon," he'd said, and she had drifted back into sleep with King by her side. She hadn't been wearing a watch, but she might have guessed that second fire stoking to be about two in the morning. If so, Jake would have a short night, because by eight she was going to be ready to haul him out of bed and head over to the main house for breakfast if he didn't come down the stairs.

Since it was light and she was awake, Holly decided to clean up quickly and take King for a walk. Once she had done that, she went back to the cabin and brewed a pot of coffee, hoping the smell would entice Jake down the stairs.

Something brought him down. Holly tried to decide if his descent was a good thing or not, as an unshaven, yawning Jake in jeans and a rumpled flannel shirt faced her. This was a new thing. She'd never seen Jake at less than his best, and just figured he was probably one of those people who bounced out of bed every morning looking as fresh as he did at eight when he came into the office. Apparently this was not the case.

"Good morning," she said, trying not to giggle or stare. His blond hair had a cowlick right at one temple that she'd never noticed before. He raised a hand in a halfhearted wave, mumbled something that might have been an answer and shuffled over to the coffeepot. "So, did you sleep well?" she asked as he sat down at the small table near the kitchenette built into one wall of the cabin.

"I slept. I woke up and it was light. And cold," he said, staring into his coffee mug in a semidazed fashion. "You're sure this isn't decaf, right?"

"Positive. Sorry there isn't any milk or anything with it, but I forgot to load up on those kinds of supplies. I'm sure Dorothy will be happy to help me out with them when we go over to the main house for breakfast."

"Great. For now black is fine." Jake took a long swallow of the burning brew. Holly wondered how he drank anything that hot, but he obviously needed the boost badly enough to drink things at the scalding level.

Half an hour of coffee and a hot shower worked magic on Jake. After all of that he looked like a slightly more casual version of the man she was used to seeing in the office in the morning. He still wore jeans and a sweater, but now his hair behaved and his eyes were bright. All his sentences made sense, too. Holly noticed he didn't even grumble about the dog sitting between them on the way to the main house.

Once they got there, Jake and King were both equally enthusiastic about breakfast. Holly was pretty sure that Jake didn't cook in that bachelor loft of his, and she didn't think he usually stopped anywhere in between there and the office for anything like this. Maybe that was why he showed such appreciation for Dorothy's flapjacks and sausages, with a couple of eggs on the side. You would think the man was going to be out riding the range, instead of in a warm cabin working on a computer, the way he was eating.

"Jake? We can come back for lunch," she said, try-ing to keep the amusement out of her voice.

"You probably will," Jake said. "Once I get in-volved with those files, I can't guarantee I'll stop."

Holly watched him keep eating breakfast. Judg-ing from the way he was eating, Jake wasn't planning to stop work until about midnight.

As it turned out, Holly had to drag him away from the computer after dark to get him back to the house for dinner. After spending the day in the same room of the cabin, Holly began to discover how much she appreciated having her own outer office next to Jake's, and not being in the same room with him at work.

He talked to himself, and favored vastly different music than she did, and tended to work out problems by getting up and loping across the space behind his desk. And to make matters worse, he did all of this while looking unbelievably attractive. Holly was beginning to see what the other associates were talking about around the Bureau. Even with all his maddening little habits, Jake was very appealing.

He'd definitely charmed Dorothy in the space of twenty-four hours. Holly knew that nobody else could get away with making her wait dinner on them. But she didn't turn a hair when Jake sauntered in the kitchen half an hour later than he'd been told to show up. Mike and the ranch hands were pretty much done eating by then, leaning back in their chairs and relaxing a little. Still, Dorothy got up and began dishing up stew and taking fresh biscuits out of the oven. In the past when Holly had been at the ranch, she'd seen tardy ranch hands told to fix their own or deal with cold dinner, but not Jake.

She wondered why nobody else groused about the special treatment he was getting, but in a few minutes she discovered the answer to that, too. "Since we have company, I made apple crisp," Dorothy said, bringing a large, still-steaming pan to the table. She set it closest to Jake, who exclaimed over the wonderful smell coming from the dessert, but nobody turned down a helping or two with the vanilla ice cream Mike found in the freezer.

When they were ready to go back to the cabin, King planted himself by Holly's side, looking hopeful. "You should stay here," she told him. The dog pawed her jeans leg gently and whined as if he understood her words and was trying to talk her into a different decision.

Mike looked at her in concern. "Are you sure you want to leave him here? You two came out here for safety. Why not provide all of it you can?"

Holly shook her head. "I know we'll be safe. Nothing unusual has gone on today, has it?"

"No." Mike looked like he hated to admit it. "I did see more than usual of the county deputies cruising when I was where I could see the road. Nobody else, though."

The dog whined again and Holly caved in. "Oh, all right, come on, then," she told King. She hugged her brother and patted the dog. "You will just have to wait until morning for your reassurance." She already had hers by trusting in the Lord, but Holly felt that explaining that one more time to anyone here would be useless. If they didn't understand it by now, she might as well save her breath, and let the dog come back to the cabin.

She went back to the kitchen to collect Jake. He was helping Dorothy clear the table and chatting with her while they worked. "Come on, Jake. The bus is leaving," she said. "Thanks for dinner, Dorothy. Everything was great, as usual. See you in the morning."

"I'll be praying for you two tonight, for safety and protection," Dorothy called out. "I'll be doing it whether you want me to or not, Jake." *So I'm not the only one trying to change Jake's heart*. The thought made her smile all the way back to the cabin.

Jake looked at the screen again, trying to focus. He had no idea how late it was, or rather by now, how early it was. Late usually meant the hours before midnight, and that had passed quite a while ago. He looked over at the fireplace and noticed that it was past time to put another log on the pile. The fire had sifted down almost to embers again. He was falling down on the job. Now that he noticed the dying fire, he could sense the chill in the room that should have told him to add another log. If it was this cool down here, right in front of the fire, what was the bedroom like? Holly was probably freezing. How did he get so wrapped up in these programs that everything else ceased to exist?

Holly had gone to bed hours ago after falling asleep twice on the couch. No sense in dragging her down here again just because she was too cold to sleep. He got up from his computer chair, stretching the kinks out of his back and shoulders on the way

over to the log basket. He put two of the smaller logs
across the embers and used the fireplace tools to re-
position them until the dying fire caught. King lifted
his head where he'd been sleeping, then relaxed again
as the fire blazed. That should keep things warmer
in the cabin for a few more hours.

He knew he should sleep, like Holly and King, but
it was so hard to think about sleeping when he was
just around the corner from the evidence he needed
to put Barclay away for good. Of course, he'd felt that
way for two or three days now, and the solution stayed
just around the corner. For once he wished that the
faith that seemed to come so easily to Holly, and to
the rest of the family, hadn't passed him by. If he was
a praying man, he'd be praying about this right now.

So why couldn't you be? He could almost hear
Holly ask him the question, even though she was upstairs asleep. And he could definitely picture what
she'd look like asking, even down to the details like
the soft flannel shirt she'd worn today, the way her
hair framed her face when she didn't pull it back in
the tight French braid, and the sparkle in her deep-
brown eyes.

Jake didn't know what startled him more, the fact
that he could picture Holly so easily answering the
question, or the fact that he was actually considering
it. What had happened to him? This trial prep and everything that went with it had turned his world up-

side down. Instead of going to the office every day he was in a cabin out in the middle of nowhere, seriously considering the power of prayer and the attractiveness of his assistant. Both were such foreign ideas to him that his head spun thinking about them.

Maybe he needed a little fresh air. Jake looked at the coatrack next to the cabin door and found his jacket. Pulling it on, he went outside and stood there, staring up at the glittering stars. He breathed in the sharp, cold air and tried to clear his head. After a few moments he decided that his head was as clear as it was going to get, and he still felt just as odd as he had before.

King barked softly when Jake came back, then quieted when Jake checked the fireplace again to make sure the fire was burning steadily. Then he took off his jacket and went over to the steep stairs to the bedroom. Climbing, he took a deep breath, trying to talk himself out of this crazy scheme one last time. It didn't work, and he found himself at the door to the bedroom, wondering whether to knock or call out or flee. He settled for knocking while he called Holly's name, and opened the door.

She sat up in bed, brushing soft waves of dark hair from her eyes. "Jake? What's the matter? Do you need me?"

"Yes, Holly, I need you." His throat tightened just looking at her, the softness of sleep still on her features in the wedge of light from the open doorway. "I hate to wake you up, but it's important. Could you come downstairs for a few minutes?"

"Sure." Her voice was still thick with sleep. "Give me a minute to put myself together and I'll be down."

"Be careful on the stairs," he said, and went down to sit on the couch and wait for her. The longer he sat on the couch, the sillier this whole idea sounded. A piece of wood popped in the fire and Jake jumped, feeling every muscle tense. What was he doing?

Then the bedroom door opened and closed and Holly came down the stair-ladder. She was in the velour sweat suit she'd slept in the night before, her hair still cascading around her face. Holly looked more beautiful and vulnerable than Jake had ever seen her look. At that moment he understood why she wore her hair pulled back at work, in order to hide from the world the look that only he could see on her face right now. His heart was beating fast as she crossed the room. "So, what is it? Did you finally break Barclay's last code?"

Jake had to push to get the words out. "No, I didn't. And that's what I need help with."

A look of confusion crossed her face. "Jake, you're the coder. I'm just the administrative assistant, remember? I can take notes or write memos or set up file copies of documents, but breaking computer code is beyond my capabilities." Her dark eyes looked so mystified, and Jake longed to reach across to her and stroke her velvet cheek in comfort.

"You have other skills too, Holly, and one of them is what I need tonight," he began, keeping his hands in his lap. "You probably won't believe what you're hearing, but I need you to show me…how to ask for help. I've been watching you through this whole crisis and you're never at a loss."

"That's because I'm not handling it myself, Jake. I turn it over to God." She idly stroked the dog, who had sat down next to her as soon as she'd come downstairs.

"Exactly," he said, willing her with a look to understand him. She still seemed puzzled, and he forced himself to go on. "You turn your problems over to God, and you make it look so natural. Show me how, Holly."

She looked at him, wide-eyed and silent for so long he wasn't sure that she'd heard him correctly. Then one lone tear coursed down her cheek and her lower lip trembled. "Of course," she said softly. "I'll show you as much as I can."

She reached out with warm, soft hands and grasped both of his, which seemed incredibly rough next to her skin. She bowed her head and those waves of heavy brown hair cascaded around her face, hiding her expression but not her words.

"Heavenly Father," she began quietly, "We're asking for Your help. Please guide Jake as he seeks to find justice for so many people, to take the power away from the drug cartel that's torn the city apart and ruined so many lives. We know that You have the power that matters, the ability to do all things that are right and good. Show Jake what's right and good in this situation, and how to defeat the darkness and evil of the drug ring that has poisoned so many lives." Then she was silent, still grasping his hands. Jake could feel the warmth of her flesh and the ring of her words around him.

He tried to form the right ones of his own. Still, he felt like a child in the dark compared to Holly when it came to prayer. It came so naturally to her, and for him it had been so very, very long since he'd even considered that there was a God who cared enough to listen just to him. "Help me, Father," he finally managed to say.

Holly took over again after that, finishing their prayer and then looking up at him with shining eyes. "Thank you, Jake. That's the best thing anybody has ever woken me up for," she said.

He nodded, dumbly. What did he say to her? Stock phrases like *You're welcome* didn't seem enough somehow for something like the gift she'd just given him. Because he felt just as confused as he had been before about breaking Barclay's last puzzle. But even though he was still in the dark, he knew he wasn't alone while he struggled. And suddenly that made all the difference in the world.

Holly sat on the couch, vaguely aware that the fire was dying and her feet, in their cotton socks, were growing colder by the minute. But the rest of her was glowing with warmth, not from the fire, or even Jake's touch, but from the joy that overwhelmed her. Jake had gotten her up in the middle of a dark, cold night to help him with work, and it was a wonderful thing. Because here, for the first time, was the kind of help she had longed to give him all along, but thought he would never ask for.

She felt like dancing, singing. Instead, she reached out impulsively and hugged him. "Jake, this is so great. I just know you're going to find the answer now," she told him. His answering hug was firm, and his stubbly cheek rasped against her skin before he let her go. She was deeply aware of his masculinity, but for the first time in years, she was comfortable with a man's touch.

Before she had time to think about the wonder of that, Jake had pulled away, and was heading toward his computer again. "I think you're right, Holly," he said over his shoulder, pulling out the chair. "If you want to stay around for good luck, or support, I'd love to have you here. King's okay, but I could use some human support. Keep me company while I work, okay?"

"Okay," she said, getting up briefly to add another

log to the fire. She settled back on the couch, pulling the blanket that was draped over the back of it around her while she watched Jake's long, slender fingers fly over the keyboard. He'd apparently been using the blanket himself at some point, because there was the hint of his cologne on it. That was a welcoming scent as she watched him murmur softly to himself…or perhaps he was beginning to talk to God on his own? Whatever the case, Holly sat wrapped in the blanket at one end of the couch, and watched him work while the glow of the moment surrounded her.

In what seemed like a few minutes Jake's hand was on her shoulder and she was trying to sit upright again after sliding down the smooth leather arm of the couch. She'd fallen asleep; that much was apparent when she opened her eyes and looked at the dying fire again. "Holly? Come on, wake up."

Jake sat on the edge of the couch, warm and smiling next to her. King sat next to him on the floor, watching the two humans. "I did it. We did it. There's enough there in the last level of hidden files to tie Barclay to La Mano Oscura and Baltasar Escalante, the plane full of drugs, everything. Nothing can stop it now."

"That's great," Holly said, leaning her head onto his welcoming shoulder. "See what happens when you ask for a little help?"

"I couldn't have done it alone," he said, nuzzling her temple. "You're an amazing woman. I never realized until all this just how amazing. Or how much a woman."

The husky tone of his voice would have sent her into a panic even a day before. But now Holly sat still in surprise at the feelings Jake was stirring in her. He was strong and masculine and exultant with power, sitting so close to her that she could feel the heat of his body covering her and she had no desire to push him away. In fact, it was all she could do not to draw him even closer. What was happening?

His lips were seeking hers now, and Holly was awash with feelings that were new and overwhelming. Her hands on the depth of his muscled chest should have been pushing him away, but she did not do so. But, as the kiss began to deepen, Holly found the little inner reserve she had left and backed away from Jake. He was still there, just inches from her.

"Jake, this is going to be even harder for me than praying was for you," she told him, pressing her lips together to keep from letting a sob escape.

"I can't believe that," he said, his words slow and honeyed. "You must not know how hard it was for me to ask for help."

"Oh, I know," she said, feeling tears prick the corners of her eyes. "And that's why it hurts so much to say this, but we have to stop now. And nothing like this can ever happen again between us." There was no way to stop the tears now, but she could keep Jake from seeing them. Holly pulled away from him, fleeing the comforting warmth of his arms as she nearly flew up the stairs to the cold bedroom. The door slammed behind her and she locked it. Daylight came before she stopped trembling enough to fall asleep.

Chapter Seven

What had happened? Jake asked himself the same question for hours and failed to get an answer that satisfied him. He ran the scene over in his mind a dozen times and remained as confused afterward as he had been when Holly fled the room. At first he thought that she'd come back down in a few minutes and they'd talk over what went on. But when that didn't happen in the first twenty minutes or so, he knew he'd lost his chance to go after her as well.

He fell asleep sitting straight up on the couch, still trying to puzzle out the answer to his question. He briefly thought about taking the question in prayer to God, but he wasn't sure he'd like the results he would get. After all, it was his rusty prayer that kicked off this whole confusing mess to begin with.

In the morning Holly came down from her bedroom and seemed distant and detached in a way she hadn't been since her first few weeks as his assistant, two years ago. She still wore jeans and a flannel shirt, but the shirt was buttoned up to the collar and tight at the cuffs. Her hair was trapped back in a French braid. She'd walked King outside without a word for Jake.

Even the folks at the main house seemed to notice that something was up when they went for breakfast. Jake caught Mike and Dorothy exchanging a look, Mike shrugging broad shoulders and Dorothy giving a brief shake of her head. Their silent communication discouraged Jake from discussing anything with either of them. He drank his coffee, ate his breakfast and the three of them went back to the cabin as silently as they'd come, dog in the middle of the front seat.

Now that he'd made the final breakthrough in Barclay's files, there was so much to do that Jake could have used two assistants. Holly did two people's work in the days that followed, but she did it so quietly and calmly that it made Jake want to scream. More than once he wanted to grasp her shoulders and make her look straight into his face while he asked her point-blank what had happened.

As much as he wanted to, he finally came to the conclusion that he couldn't do that. Something kept holding him back, though he couldn't say just what it was. All he knew for sure was that he and Holly had shared something incredibly special that changed the way he looked at life, and at her. And now he couldn't bring back that magic moment, much as he tried.

It really did a number on his newfound faith to think that this glorious sense of trust in God that had developed might come at the price of his growing relationship with Holly. Why couldn't he have both? If God was the awesome all-powerful being that Holly had said He was, why weren't all the pieces of Jake's life coming together at the same time? He'd asked for help, and gotten it so quickly that it was like one of those heavenly lightning bolts you see in cartoons. But just as quickly the flames of the fire that had sparked between him and Holly had gone out. It still didn't make sense.

Friday morning Jake looked around the cabin as he drank his coffee. This was the last day he and Holly would be here together. It was Christmas Eve, and the trial prep was basically over. Tomorrow he'd be back in the city with his family, celebrating the holiday. For the first time in years he actually looked forward to going to church with his parents. That would surprise them all.

He'd talked to Rose half a dozen times this week, whenever cell phone reception and time allowed them to grab a moment. "I look for jury selection to be over by Monday noon and opening statements that afternoon. You'll be up by Wednesday, Thursday at the latest," she told him. And now, he was ready.

Jake took another drink of his coffee. It was growing cold. He should feel on top of the world. The biggest case of his career was working out better than he could have hoped. After years of feeling detached from his family because he just couldn't share the faith they all seemed to have in common, he had a real idea of what being a child of God was all about.

Instead of exulting over these things, Jake felt flat. He'd come to the cabin with only two objectives in mind: putting Barclay behind bars, and protecting Holly while he did so. He'd accomplished one of those things but felt as if he'd failed miserably at the other. Who knew that protecting Holly would mean he should have protected her from him? The distant, wounded look she wore now was worse than her expression after she'd been sideswiped in the street, and this time Jake had no idea of how to make things better.

She was still so efficient and competent, ready to meet his every need as long as it wasn't emotional. And as if to underscore that point, the bedroom door opened above him, and he heard her come down the ladder. After a few moments in the bathroom, she emerged looking as put together and proper as she had for the past four days, and every bit as remote. Jake was seized by the desire to throw his coffee mug across the room in frustration. If it wouldn't have startled the dog, he would have done it.

Instead he took a deep breath and stood up. "Holly, we have to talk. I'm not saying it has to happen right now, but sometime today, before we leave here, I have to know why you're avoiding me." It took most of his strength to say things as neutrally as possible instead of pulling her to him or raising his voice.

Fortunately, the restraint worked. Holly nodded slowly. "You deserve to know that much. Give me a couple hours."

He felt a pang of remorse. "Take the whole day if you need it. Can we agree to meet here after dinner, when everything is packed up, but before we go back to spend Christmas with our families?"

She nodded again. "We can. I'll give you an answer then." When she looked up at him, Jake almost changed his mind. Her deep-brown eyes sparkled with tears, and he could see that this was costing her plenty. But he'd gone too far to back down now, and he didn't think he could go back to the city without knowing why Holly had run so hot and cold in the course of an hour. That time now felt like one of the most momentous hours of his life, and he wanted to understand just how it had happened.

Holly watched Jake turn and walk away and she wondered how she was going to find the courage to keep the promise she had just made. Jake deserved an answer. Now if only she could figure out what the truth really was. The truth of her past was easy enough to explain. It wasn't pretty, but after five years she could lay out the facts of what had happened to her. What was still confusing her was what had happened three days ago, and her deep reaction to it. How did she explain to Jake how she felt? She'd thought about it and prayed about it ever since and still didn't have a concrete answer. That was the reason she'd put him off one more time, wondering what she was going to say.

Until then there was plenty to do. Everything needed to be packed up and stowed in the Jeep, and the two of them needed to go over the facts of Jake's findings on Barclay. It would take most of the day to accomplish those two things, and Mike expected them to have meals at the house in between. With it being Christmas Eve, Dorothy had probably gotten all kinds of things together to make the day a special one. Holly hoped she could at least pretend to do justice to some of Dorothy's goodies. She was already getting searching looks from Michael's housekeeper due to her lack of appetite and enthusiasm these last few days. All she needed now was someone else concerned about her.

Late tonight, if everything went as planned, Holly would go back to the main house with King and Jake would climb into the Jeep and drive it back to Colorado Springs to get his newly repaired vehicle and join his family for whatever they had planned for Christmas. Neither of them had talked much about Christmas Day in this wild week of trial preparation and personal contact. All Holly knew for sure was that once they got back to the city again, she and Jake faced a week focused on the trial, not each other.

If they were going to resolve any of these things between them, it would have to be today. But first, there was so much to do, most of it together. Holly took a deep breath, squared her shoulders, and began praying under her breath. It was the only way she could imagine getting through a day like this one promised to be.

Nine hours later everything was packed and stowed in the Jeep except the barest of essentials. They'd gone over the trial information twice. Holly was so proud of Jake and the work he'd done, and the fact that he'd found a way to ask God for help in doing it. That surprised her so much more than anything else that happened in their week together. Even their tumultuous kiss days before wasn't as big a shock as that prayer.

Now she was nearly weaving on her feet from the day's work. Looking around the compact bedroom in the cabin one last time, she checked for anything she might have left behind. Or maybe she just stalled for time to keep from facing Jake yet. There was so little space in the bedroom that the latter seemed more likely. The neatly made bed, rustic chest of drawers with a battery-operated clock on top, and one rag rug under a straight-backed chair still made up the only furniture in the room. None of her belongings could hide in a room like this, and it was time for her to stop hiding as well. She turned off the light and went down the stairs.

Jake sat on the couch in front of the sofa, poking at the embers of the dying fire. Midwinter darkness had begun to gather outside the windows, and on any other evening Holly would have been touched by the tray of cocoa and cookies that he'd somehow put together for their last hour in the cabin. It was a thoughtful gesture, and one she knew hadn't come naturally to him.

He looked up, and saw her gaze at the tray sitting on top of the leather ottoman. "It was the least I could do," he said with a gesture. "Neither of us drinks alcohol, so there was no sense in suggesting a little Dutch courage to get through this, whatever it's going to be. We'll just have to make do with hot cocoa."

Holly nodded in agreement and made her way to the sofa, sitting on the other end from Jake. "Thank you. How did you put this together, anyway?"

He shrugged. "It's nothing fancy. The cocoa's instant, made with water from the coffeemaker. Even I can do that. And I conned Dorothy out of the cookies when we were there for lunch. I thought it might be nice to have something here to take the edge off our discussion. If anything can." In the course of his speech, Jake's face had gone from a boyish grin to a more somber look as he watched Holly's face. "So. You were going to explain everything to me. Is there any way I can make things easier?"

Holly shook her head. "I don't think anybody could. It's kind of you to try, Jake."

"Kindness. One of the many traits you wouldn't have expected from me before this week, huh?" His blue eyes held an intense gleam. "There have been a lot of unexpected things for me this week, Holly. I never expected to find faith of the kind my parents seem to have so naturally The fact that I found it here with you, even if it's only the beginnings of faith, has knocked me for a loop."

"I can tell," she began, thanking God for the transition Jake's admission provided. "And it's knocked me for a loop too, to use your phrase. This whole week has been intense and filled with the unexpected. For me the most unexpected thing was that I found myself in your arms, and I liked it." She took a deep breath, closing her eyes briefly. There. The hardest part of this had begun. Now if she could just rely on the strength she knew her Heavenly Father had, and trust Him to put the right words in her mouth, maybe this would all go well after all.

"You liked it?" Jake's brow knit. "It sure didn't look that way. You were up those stairs faster than summer lightning."

"I was scared and shocked. I still am."

Jake drew back a little, looking confused. "Am I that scary? Funny, I've always been told I had quite a touch...."

Holly stopped Jake before he could go further. "No, not just by your advances. By my reaction to them. Responding that warmly to that kind of attention from you was the last thing I expected to do." She found herself clutching the mug of cocoa like a life preserver. Its comforting warmth gave her something to focus on besides the discomfort of what lay ahead. Even King seemed to sense her unease, whining from his spot on the rug.

She took a tiny sip of the warm liquid, all she could manage. There was no way to put things nicely and make Jake understand how conflicted her feelings were. "How much do you know about my life before I started working for the FBI, and for you?"

"Very little. I recognized your name when you interviewed, because I know plenty of your extended family. Your mom taught me English in high school, but she taught almost everybody of our generation who went to the public high school. I vaguely remember that you went to college out of state, and lived there for a while afterward. Why?"

"Mainly because of things that happened when I was still in Ohio, after finishing school there. I liked Ohio, thought I'd stay there forever. With my business degree I got a nice job and enjoyed it. I was active in a good church with a fun singles group, and the money I made was enough to let me look at buying a condo in one of the nicer suburbs of Cincinnati. And then along came Victor Convy."

"Bad dating relationship?"

"It was worse than that, I'm afraid." Holly tried to keep her hands from trembling as she spoke. She finally put down the cup, sure that if she held it longer, the cocoa would slosh out. "Victor started going to the singles group at my church. It was one of those large megachurches and there were over thirty of us in the group. He didn't seem like the normal church-group kind of guy, but I decided to give him a chance when he asked me out.

"We went out twice by ourselves outside of the church group. Victor was older that I was by a few years, and even though he tossed around what seemed like a lot of money, he appeared lonely, somehow. The first time, we went to a restaurant that was far nicer than anyplace I would have gone by myself, or with my friends from work. He asked me what kind of music I liked, and when I said classical he told me that he had two tickets to the symphony the next week. When he invited me to go along, I agreed."

"Sounds like a perfectly nice guy. Why am I already suspicious?" Jake sounded as protective as Mike and Ken, which touched Holly's heart, and made her hate to continue her story. But it was too late to stop now.

"The symphony was great. Victor knew I didn't drink, so he made a great show of going somewhere for just coffee and dessert afterward. He insisted that I get a fancy flavored coffee drink. Halfway through it I felt odd and ill. My first instinct was to call a taxi, but Victor insisted on taking me home."

"I don't like where this is going," Jake said. Holly looked down to see that his knuckles were white where he grasped his mug of hot chocolate. "He slipped something in your coffee, didn't he? If you don't want to tell me any more, I can guess the rest."

"You could, but I'm ready to tell you now." Holly felt close to tears, moved by his concern and anger. "He took me to his home instead of the apartment I shared with another woman from work. My memory was hazy, and I seemed to be unable to make it as clear as I was trying to that I didn't want the attention he was forcing on me. He raped me and afterward took me home to my apartment and dropped me off at the front of the building, still feeling sick and groggy, barely able to get the door unlocked."

"Did you call the police?" Jake's eyes were a steely blue that looked frightening.

"It was the first thing I did once I could get my thoughts together enough to dial the phone. I went through a night in the emergency room, giving my statement, all the awful things rape victims have to do if they want their attacker prosecuted. And I certainly wanted him prosecuted. Even if I had been reluctant, I probably would have continued because the police urged me to do it. One female detective told me that there were at least three other women she was aware of personally who had accused Convy of date rape."

"But he wasn't ever charged? Brought to trial?"

"Not before that. He was a wealthy man with good lawyers and a knack for picking vulnerable women. No one else pressed charges."

"But you did." It wasn't a question, just a flat statement, and Holly echoed it.

"I did. The prosecutor at the time really argued for me to stay strong and see it through. He warned me that if I didn't, Convy would be back on the street doing this again. And I think he saw me as the perfect victim to take Convy down. I was twenty-four, a devout Christian and everybody who knew me well knew I wouldn't have gone to Convy's apartment that night of my own free will, much less have ever agreed to have sex with him. My faith, and the beliefs it entailed, wasn't any secret to my friends then, Jake, any more than it is now."

"Did you win? Is he in jail?"

"We won, and Convy went to jail. The funny thing was that I felt like I went to jail along with him, just a different kind of jail."

"I can only imagine. How long did you stay in Cincinnati after the trial?"

"Four months. No matter where I went, it felt like people were staring. Everybody at work knew, my singles group at church, my roommate, everyone. All the plans I'd made before felt flat. Buying my own place was out of the question, because I no longer had any desire to live alone. My family was very supportive, but they all kept saying that I should come home and make a fresh start. When, on top of everything else my father's cancer became terminal, I knew it was time to come home."

For a moment the room was silent except for the popping and hissing of the dying fire. After a long while, Jake spoke. "Have you had any serious relationships since you came home?" His tone was quiet and searching.

"None. It was hard just to go back to church at first, or do anything social. I haven't been on anything you'd call a date in close to five years. So I guess you can see why having you take me in your arms startled me."

"To say the least."

She looked over to the other end of the sofa. Jake had put down his mug and was staring at the cooling embers in the fireplace. "So can you understand why I said this can't happen again?"

"I can. Will you accept my apologies? If I'd have known…"

His tone sounded like pity, and that was the last thing she ever wanted from Jake Montgomery. "There was no way you could have known, Jake." She got up off the sofa, feeling cold and stiff in the darkening room. "Now why don't we clear this up and start heading toward the house? The cocoa is cold and it's time to go. Your family will expect you home tonight."

Jake nodded and began gathering up the untouched cookie tray and the mugs. It didn't take long to have the cabin back to the state it had been when they first entered it. Holly looked around the room from the doorway. *What a way to spend Christmas Eve,* she thought.

Jake came up beside her and scanned the room. "That's it, then." He stood for a moment looking into her eyes, then opened his mouth. He said nothing for the longest time, just standing there, looking at her, his hands gently on her shoulders. "No, that's it, then," he said again softly and led her outside. Holly hoped that in the darkness he couldn't see the tears she knew were glittering unshed in her eyes.

* * *

Jake felt like an utter, absolute fool. How could he have pressed himself on Holly? Given what she'd been through, it must have seemed like a terrible repeat of old nightmares. Here he was, looking like another wealthy, casual guy out for a good time at her expense. He wondered how long it would be before he could tell her all the things he wanted to tell her, now that he'd heard her story. Maybe once they got back to Colorado Springs…and maybe never.

His throat was so tight right now he could barely force words out. It would be quite a while before he'd be able to tell her how much this week meant to him, especially knowing what he did now about the beautiful woman sitting silently beside him as they drove the back roads of the ranch toward the house.

He was going to miss the quiet of working just with Holly and King in the cabin. Tomorrow he'd be surrounded by his family and by Sunday afternoon or evening, he knew that Rose was going to want to hear everything he had to say in preparation for the trial next week. Their time of relative peace at the ranch was over. As if to underscore that, they pulled up in front of the house where all the lights shone brightly and several cars and trucks clustered outside on the gravel drive.

"I'll come in for a few minutes," Jake said. "Help you carry in your things."

There was a pause when he expected to hear Holly argue, but then she just said, "Okay. Thanks," and started taking her suitcases from the back of the Jeep. "That box in the corner there is full of wrapped presents. If you want to carry that in, it would help."

Jake nodded and did as he was told, marveling again at the forethought Holly had shown. While he was planning what files to bring this week she had been looking ahead to Christmas and wrapping her family's gifts. He looked down at the contents of the box, conscious that he had a few problems in that category. While he'd had Holly take care of his mother's present, he had fallen down on the job with everybody else. Here it was, late on Christmas Eve and he was presentless for virtually everybody he knew.

As he followed Holly into the warm, brightly lit house, she motioned toward the living room, where a magnificent tree stood near the fieldstone fireplace. "Just set them down there and I'll put them where they belong later," she told him.

She disappeared around the corner with her suitcases, and Jake could hear her calling to Dorothy and Mike. Then there were the happy noises of King and Molly bounding down a hallway toward each other, in greeting. Holly and King came back into the living room. "If you look in the Jeep in the same corner of the back that you just took that box from, you'll find another one," she told him. "I took the liberty while I was shopping to do a little more with you in mind. I didn't wrap anything in case what I chose doesn't suit you, but I think you'll find gifts for Adam and Kate, your father and Colleen."

"Wow. You really are amazing, do you know that?" Jake was surprised at Holly's reaction. She looked away from him, bending down to pay attention to King.

"Nowhere near amazing, Jake. But I am a good shopper, and I've seen how wrapped up in the Barclay information you've been. There's one small thing that's already wrapped and has a tag on it. My gift to you. Nothing much." She was still looking at the dog while she talked to Jake.

Jake started beating himself up mentally. Not only did he have nothing for Holly, but he had no way to tell her that he'd already gotten more in the way of gifts from her than he could ever repay. "You really shouldn't have done that," he said, aware of how lame it sounded even as he spoke.

"Well, I did, so it's done," Holly said firmly, looking up at him again. "Now come in and say goodbye, so that you can get on the road before it gets too late."

Dutifully he followed her into the kitchen, where Dorothy and Mike sat in the kitchen, along with Holly's mother. "Good to see you again," he told Marilyn, meaning it this time.

"And it's good to see you, too, Jake. Merry Christmas," Mrs. Vance said.

He passed on Dorothy's offer of any more food or visiting, telling everyone he needed to get on the road and get back for his family Christmas, which was more than true.

"I'll walk you out," Mike told him, the two of them going out the back door before Holly could protest, and walking around the house together, but alone.

"The county sheriff's trucks have been cruising by the ranch on a regular basis," Mike said. "I don't know what you two are involved in, but it's obviously serious."

"It is, but nothing I can't handle," Jake said, wishing he felt that confident about all the trouble he'd caused Holly. At least about the stalker, he felt that nothing would come along now that he couldn't handle, anyway.

"I can keep an eye on her tonight, and tomorrow, but once you two are back in the city, I expect you to look after Holly." Mike had a serious expression Jake could read even in the faint light that came through the windows of the house.

"Don't worry. I won't let her out of my sight until she's safe at home. And I've got a few other things in mind that will keep her even safer," he told Mike, mentally noting that he needed to call Mike's cousin Peter Vance and see if Peter's brother Travis still had the range of private investigation hardware he'd known him to have in the past.

"See that you do," Mike said, clapping a hand on your shoulder. "Now I believe we're about to get company." They were to the front of the house now, and Holly stood there with King by her side. Calling to his dog, Mike went inside to let them say their goodbyes.

After what they'd been through in the last hour, Jake was afraid to touch Holly. He stood in front of her, anxious to get on the road, unsure of how much to say. His nerve failed him. "I'll see you Sunday, right?"

"Right. Drive carefully."

"I will." He headed to the Jeep, having one last thought that made him stop and look at Holly again. "Plan on a long time with Rose. She's ruthless."

Holly rolled her eyes. "I already know that. She's my cousin, remember? You should see what she's like at Scrabble." And on that lighter note they parted and Jake felt any chance of telling Holly what was on his mind evaporate.

Chapter Eight

"All right, what's up?" Marilyn Vance plopped herself down beside her daughter on Mike's worn couch. Like most of the furniture on the ranch, the couch was old and well loved. It was a comfortable spot to seek solace, and Holly had been doing just that. Even in this sprawling ranch house, though, she could only hide from her mother so long.

"You barely touched dinner. And you looked like you were on automatic pilot at church, when eleven o'clock on Christmas Eve is usually your favorite service of the year. I know this had to be a hard week, Holly, but just being tired doesn't account for the way you look tonight."

Holly shook her head. "You're right, Mom. I'm a lot more than just tired. It *was* a long, hard week and that's part of it. But there's a lot more to things than that. Things came up between us in the course of the week, and just before we left the cabin in the afternoon, I told Jake about Victor Convy."

"What did he say? And why did you tell him? It's not the kind of thing I'd think your boss would have to know about."

Holly pulled the blanket that was usually draped over the back of the couch tighter around her shoulders. She'd been cold since leaving the cabin, and the nubby wool was a comfort. "He didn't say much afterward. He looked angry, not at me, but at Convy, and just…I don't know, at life, somehow. He's seen a lot as an FBI agent, and I guess this is just one more confirmation that there are a lot of bad people out there."

Marilyn Vance shook her head. "We all knew that already. And I have to suspect that it wasn't something related to your work, even prosecuting somebody like Alistair Barclay, that led to this decision to tell Jake about what happened in Ohio." Her mother took her hand, and Holly was surprised to find how warm her mother's hand was, and how cool her own felt in comparison.

"You're right again. I think I've gone and fallen in love with Jake, which is impossible," she said, trying not to cry. "And until tonight he might have had some kind of feelings for me, although with Jake it's hard to tell. He kissed me the other day, Mom, and I liked it. A lot."

"That's wonderful. I've been praying for five years that some man would find a way to give you back what that monster stole from you."

"Mom, we both know that I can't get back what Convy stole," Holly said softly.

"No, I don't just mean what he took physically. I mean your confidence in yourself, and your feelings as a woman. He stole those, too, you know. But they can be returned." They sat together for quite a while in silence, and then Marilyn turned to face her daughter. "Now, since it's obvious that neither of us will go to sleep for a while, please explain to me why it's impossible for you to be in love with Jake Montgomery. Frankly, I couldn't think of a better candidate to be in love with, if he'd just settle down a little."

"That's just it," Holly said, working hard so that her words didn't come out as a wail. "If Jake wanted to settle down, wouldn't he do it with one of the dozen or more cute, rich little blondes that he's dated on and off for years?"

"Nonsense. I went to school with his mother, all the way from kindergarten on up, and I can only imagine what a sensible woman like Liza Kinally would have said if her son would have brought home one of those silly little girls and announced that she was going to be his future bride."

Somehow her mother's statement struck her as the funniest thing that she'd heard in a week, but Holly tried not to laugh because she could see that Marilyn was perfectly serious. She honestly thought that Jake would put that much store in what his mother felt about his choice of a wife. But then, before she opened her mouth, memories of Jake's actions came back to her. He did care about pleasing his mother. That much was clear in the fact that hers was the only Christmas present he'd made an effort to secure before their work on the trial. And Liza was a serious, godly woman. Maybe her mother had a point after all.

"I still think that the one who has the final say in whom Jake Montgomery marries will be no one but Jake," Holly said.

"And that's as it should be. I didn't mean to imply otherwise," her mom said. "But tell the truth, now. If you were in Jake's shoes, who would you rather take home to mother? One of those interchangeable blondes from the society pages, or a nice girl like you?"

Spoken like a true mother, Holly thought. At least this discussion with her mom was lifting her spirits. Sitting here with her mom patting her knee, she felt better than she expected she would. Maybe things weren't quite as dark as they'd seemed in the cabin after all.

* * *

Christmas Day dawned bright and clear. Jake felt as chilled as the crisp, sparkling landscape outside when he left his loft to join the rest of the family at Good Shepherd. After spending a little over a week with Holly in a space far smaller than his apartment, the loft felt huge, cold and empty. What had previously looked like spare, clean lines in decorating seemed stark now, especially since there wasn't a single Christmas decoration of any kind, unless you counted the pile of cards other people had sent him. They lay strewn on his glass-topped coffee table, providing the one note of color.

He walked out into the cold air with his small box of presents. It was so incredibly thoughtful of Holly to do his shopping, and even more thoughtful of her to leave everything unwrapped, yet provide the wrapping paper, tape and scissors in the box so that he could put things together. Jake decided she knew him all too well at this point, since she could predict that he would have left the shopping for everybody else until it was too late. At the same time, Holly was still a mystery to him in so many important ways. Maybe when this trial was over in a week or two, he could start working on exploring those mysteries. He hoped so, anyway. For now he had to focus on Christmas morning without her.

The one bright note to the morning was anticipating his mother's face. What would she say when he walked into church on time, even a little bit early, wearing a suit and smiling? It was worth the struggle to get up and dressed and load everything into Holly's Jeep just to see the look of surprise he knew his mom would have.

Liza didn't disappoint him. Her smile rivaled her new daughter-in-law Kate's for brilliance in the crowded church. All three of the women in Jake's newly enlarged family hugged him after he slipped into the pew where they were gathered.

"A suit?" his sister Colleen said, just above a whisper. "And showing up for services without a reminder call or anything? You sure you aren't sick, Jake?"

"Not in the least. In fact, I don't know when I've felt better," he told her, smiling back. It was always fun to leave Colleen mystified. Her reporter's curiosity would drive her nuts now for the rest of the day, just trying to figure out what he was up to.

He shook hands with his father and Adam, glad to see that Adam's return handshake and shoulder clap were heartier now than they'd been even a month ago. He seemed to be over any lasting effects of his gunshot wound earlier in the year. "You're coming back for Christmas dinner, aren't you?" his mother asked once he settled into the pew.

"Sure. I wouldn't miss it," he said, wondering what prompted that question. He hadn't missed a holiday dinner of any kind at his parents' house since he'd moved out over a decade before.

The slight look of worry his mother's eyes had held cleared. "Good. When I saw you here, I thought maybe you were working so hard on the case that you were coming to church instead of spending the rest of the day with us."

He took his mother's small, soft hand and squeezed it. "Mom, if you can believe it, I'm here because I want to be. Because I felt like coming to join the rest of you here in God's house to celebrate the day."

He wasn't prepared for the tears that sprang to her eyes, even though her smile was more brilliant than before. "Jake, you don't know how long I've prayed to hear just that from you. No matter what else you got me for Christmas, it won't compare to the gift you just gave me." She leaned over quickly and kissed him on the cheek, then settled back into her seat.

The organ music swelled just then, and there was no time for a reply as the Christmas Day services at Good Shepherd got under way. So Jake sat silently and mulled over the fact that he had yet another thing to thank Holly for when he saw her tomorrow. The list was growing to such proportions that he was going to need an entire candlelit dinner after Barclay's trial simply to tell her all of them.

Jake truly hadn't realized what a stranger he'd been around Good Shepherd until he met Reverend

Dawson on the way out of the church. The handsome minister, greeting people in the narthex after the service, shook Jake's hand warmly, then looked around behind him. "Funny, I don't see any ghosts. And you didn't bring Tiny Tim either." He looked over at Jake's mother, who was talking with Kate several people down the line to greet him. "Or did you arrange your son's appearance, Mrs. Montgomery?"

"Hey, Pastor Gabriel, this is all my own doing," Jake said, grinning over the Scrooge reference the man had made. "And you can count on seeing plenty of me from now on. I can't make a promise about every week, because of job travel, but I want to see a lot more of the inside of this place."

"Great. I look forward to it."

"So do I," said his mother firmly, from her position next to Jake where she'd caught up with him in line. "Merry Christmas, Gabriel. Your daughters look very pretty in their Christmas dresses."

"And can probably hardly wait to go home and get into something more comfortable," the pastor said with a smile, looking over at Hannah and Sarah in their velvet creations.

"I'll agree with them on that score," Liza said cheerfully. "I have a pair of slippers with jingle bells on them that I'm going to swap for these pumps the minute I get in the door at home."

Jake knew she would, too. His mother was very

formal and put-together outside the house in her roles as civic leader, mayor's wife and benefactor to the various charities around town, especially the Galilee Women's Shelter, but she didn't stand on ceremony once she was home. Ten minutes after all the cars were parked on the big circular drive of the house, Liza was wearing her slippers, and a fancy Christmas apron over her dress, and shuttling between last-minute chores in the kitchen and making sure his father had lit the huge Christmas tree where Jake, Adam and Colleen were all unloading boxes and bags of presents for the family.

"Wow, two surprises in one morning," Colleen said, motioning toward Jake's neatly wrapped pile of gifts. "Since when do you get time off work to shop?"

"I had a little help," Jake said, unwilling to say more, but needing to tell the truth to his sister, even if it was only a partial explanation.

"Cool. I hope it's the same help that got you to church this morning. I wouldn't mind seeing both of you wild men settled down, you know," Colleen said, with more fervor than Jake thought possible. His sister, with her spiky hair, and sharp attitude, a closet romantic? It made his head spin.

Jake knew that if he stayed long enough after dinner and presents, his mother would find him for a chat. Early in the day that sounded like something to be avoided, but by the time Colleen had left for a short shift at the newspaper and Adam, Kate and his father had settled in to start a round of the board game Frank had gotten for Christmas, Jake welcomed the chance to help his mom clean up the last of the dinner dishes.

Liza Montgomery could have had servants and caterers to handle occasions like Christmas dinner, but she didn't bother with anything that pretentious. Several years since his father had been elected mayor, the family had foregone Christmas dinner altogether to work together at one of the missions or centers for the homeless, serving dinner there. Until this year Jake had just figured that was a good public relations ploy on his father's part, but now, with the mustard seed of faith growing inside him, he thought it might be something else.

This year it had been nice to have dinner as a family without any other interference. He would have enjoyed spending part of the day with Holly, but she was still in Cripple Creek and he was here in town, and for the present their relationship had to stay that of boss and assistant, anyway.

"I'd offer you a penny for those thoughts, but it looks like they're of the heavier variety," his mother said, nudging him so that he noticed the dishes piling up in the sink in front of him, waiting to be dried.

"Yeah, you're right," he agreed. "I'm trying to

figure out how to get my assistant to date me without losing the best office help I've ever had."

"You can't have everything," his mother said succinctly, pulling the stopper on the sink. "Which would you rather have, a good assistant, or the company of a good woman like Holly Vance?"

"For the next week I'll have to settle for a good assistant. We're too deep into the trial prep to do anything else. But once that's over, I've got to come up with a way to change our relationship. That is, if Holly will let me." He frowned down at the dish he was drying, wondering how much to tell his mother. He couldn't betray any of Holly's confidences, but he needed advice from someone like his mother on how to best proceed here.

As if she'd read his mind, his mom stopped rubbing hand lotion into her hands and looked up at him. "Holly's an incredible woman, you know, Jake. The talks I've heard her give to some of the clients at the women's shelter have demonstrated a faith far beyond most women her age." Liza's green eyes searched his face, trying to discern how much to say.

"She told me about things that happened in Cincinnati," Jake said, knowing that he wouldn't be revealing anything from his statement that Holly hadn't already said. "How much do you know about her life there?"

"Most of what there is to tell, I expect. But given

the context in which I've heard her story, it wasn't something I could share with you as her boss." His respect for his mother grew at that moment, if it was possible to have any more respect for her than he already had. "I figured that she would share that some day, when she was ready. What moved her to the point of readiness?" she asked, succinct as always.

"We've been working very closely on this trial. And working out on her brother's ranch we got even closer. One night I ended up taking her in my arms, and my emotions got the best of me when we kissed. I don't feel very good about that. If I'd known what I know now, it never would have happened."

"Perhaps it was supposed to happen, Jake." His mother's voice was soft, yet confident. "I don't believe in too many coincidences in the Christian life. I believe God puts us in certain situations for good reasons, even though they're beyond our understanding. Maybe that was one of those times. Would you be willing to entertain that possibility?"

"I guess so. It certainly isn't any stranger than anything else I've seen or thought about in the last few weeks, including being willing to consider that God is working in my life to begin with."

"Good." His mother put an arm around him for a brief hug. "And I'll keep praying that He goes on working in your life, and you stay just as open to that work."

"Mom, I can't think of anybody else I'd rather

have praying for me," he said, meaning every word of it. Well, perhaps there was one other person he'd love to have praying for him, but he wasn't sure she'd be praying for him all that much in the near future.

On Sunday afternoon, Holly drove to Rose's office, feeling oddly nervous about seeing Jake. By the time she got to the office, Jake and Rose were deep in conversation about the evidence from Barclay's computer, with Jake going over the data. "Try to explain it to me as if I'd never done more with a computer but turn it on and perhaps check my e-mail or play solitaire," she could hear Rose saying.

"That's going to be hard," Jake grumbled. "Surely we can assume a higher degree of computer literacy on the jury pool than that."

"Surely we can't," Rose said. "It would be great if we got more, but it certainly isn't something we can count on. In fact, there will probably be at least one in the twelve or fourteen, with the alternates, who doesn't even go that far."

She looked up to the doorway where Holly stood. "Hi, there. Come on in and try to help your boss out. He needs it."

"She's got that right," Jake said, pulling out the chair next to him. "You have any ideas on how to explain this simply?"

"Hey, if she could teach you to make coffee, she

can explain this, no problem," Rose cracked, giving Jake a sassy grin. Holly had to hide one of her own in answer. It wasn't fair for both of them to pick on Jake at the same time. He already looked frustrated enough.

Holly sat down next to Jake, aware of her closeness to his long, rangy body in the next chair. He looked as good in his khakis and sweater as he would have in the suit he usually wore to work. She'd enjoyed seeing Jake in casual clothes for a week. Tomorrow morning in the office it would be strange to see him with his standard white shirt and conservative tie again. But of course he'd be wearing them, because the trial would start before day's end and they'd both be going to court.

Sitting there, Holly had an idea. "How about trying to explain the evidence on the same level that you explained to Aunt Lidia how to work the ordering system on the café's computer terminals? You did that just fine."

Jake's smile brightened. "Yeah, I did, didn't I? And the two of us were facing the double barrier of your aunt's reluctance to touch the computer and the fact that she says she still thinks in Italian, although her English is better than anybody's I know."

"Except Aunt Marilyn's," Rose added, wrinkling her nose. Holly's mother was the only person ever to give Rose a challenge in Scrabble.

"Yeah, but Holly's mom probably has better computer skills than this theoretical juror we're using, given that she works for the newspaper. From what my sister says about things at the *Sentinel*, everybody is computer literate down there."

"She's right. I'd definitely go with Aunt Lidia as a model here," Holly said. She watched Jake think about the problem, running one hand through his already rumpled blond hair. Now there was a task she'd like to help him with, she thought. It almost made her blush to consider it. After talking to her mother yesterday, she wasn't going to totally give up on Jake yet. First they had to get through the trial, and then they could think about other things.

"Jake, you coming up with a plan here?" Rose did everything but poke him across the desk. "We've got a lot to cover in a few hours, and I'd like to go home eventually."

"I'm sure you would," Jake muttered. "We've all got a big day tomorrow. How much of this is your boss letting you handle, anyway?"

"Your testimony is the biggest thing," Rose said. "That in itself is a huge deal, because after the preliminary stuff you've given me, Kirk is sure that you're going to blow the defense out of the water." She stood and stretched. "I could use another cup of coffee. Any other takers?"

Holly demurred, but Jake took her up on her offer, and Rose went into the outer office to pour two mugs.

"Thanks for returning my Jeep in such good condition," Holly told Jake while Rose was gone. "If I didn't know better, I would have said it had been washed and detailed."

"Just a little quick touch-up in my parents' driveway," Jake said. "And there's one other thing I need to tell you about it, while we're on the subject—"

"Okay, here's the coffee, with cream, no sugar. And I thought of a way to explain these layers of codes and passwords to a jury," Rose began, putting down Jake's mug as she talked rapidly. Whatever Jake was going to say about the Jeep got lost in the shuffle. In moments they were deep in conversation as the three of them bent their heads over Jake's reams of testimony for the trial that would begin in earnest in the morning.

Chapter Nine

On Monday morning Jake hardly had time to take his coat off and settle in before he had a small squabble with Holly. "I should probably stay here and keep things going while you go to the trial," she said, looking around the office.

Jake shook his head. "Not a chance, Holly. Not that much is going to happen in the next two days. The time between Christmas and New Year's isn't that busy to begin with. Everybody who could find a way to stay home this week will do so. And until I'm positive that Barclay's hired help has given up, I'm not letting you out of my sight during daylight hours."

"I hadn't thought about that part. Do you think there's still somebody out there?" Holly looked more worried than she had in several days. Jake almost felt bad for bringing up the stalker. Still, it was important, and he was already uncomfortable just letting her drive to and from the office alone.

"I can't say for certain that there isn't. Just because we've had two days back in town without him latching on to me, or you, doesn't mean he's given up. Until the trial is over and Barclay's in prison someplace, I'm not going to rest easy."

Jake didn't tell her that he wouldn't truly rest easily on this subject until they'd hauled somebody in on charges, but they didn't have to go into that now. For now he needed a little help getting the last-minute things ready for the trial, and then they'd go over to the courthouse. "Have you talked to Rose or Kirk yet this morning?" Holly asked.

"They're planning to make opening statements before the noon recess, so we need to get over there soon," Jake said. "And I do mean *we*. No more arguments about staying here, okay?"

"If you say so. I do want to see you testify, anyway. And I want to see Rose in her lawyer mode," Holly admitted. "I haven't gotten a chance to do that very often, and it's quite a show."

"I can imagine. Was she this, uh, focused as a kid?"

"Always. My mother told my uncle by the time she was eleven that he might as well plan on sending her to law school, because she could argue the leg off the dining room table." It was fun seeing

Holly grin with the memories. "Of course I suspect my mother would have gone to law school herself if teaching English hadn't been the much more acceptable route in the 1960s."

Jake shook his head. "I can only imagine the terror she would have struck in an entire generation of lawbreakers. Of course, she did that in her own way, didn't she?"

Holly sighed. "She still does. She takes the copy editors to task from the reception desk of the *Sentinel* if they mess up on anything and she finds it. But enough of this family stuff. You need to get ready to go to court. What can I do before we leave besides make sure the portfolio of printouts is in order?"

"That should do it," Jake said. "Stick your head in my office no later than ten-thirty, will you? I want to make sure my tie's on straight and I'm presentable before we head over there."

Now it was Holly's turn to shake her head. "Oh, you're always presentable, Jake. That's the least of your worries. But I'll come in at ten-thirty anyway."

She left his office and Jake could hear her computer click and whirr as she turned it on and busied herself with work. He looked back at the screen saver in front of him, trying to remember what he'd been doing before. He'd called up a search engine to do something.... What was it?

Looking at the screen, he thought for a moment,

then remembered. He was going to track down that creep in Ohio to make sure he wouldn't be adding to their woes any time soon. After a few tries he found the database for the Ohio Department of Corrections, and got to their tracking program, where he had to enter a name. Now was the time when he wished he'd taken a minute to write down the name she'd mentioned. He should have done it the moment they separated Christmas Eve, because Jake knew even then that he wanted to track this guy down and make sure he was behind bars. Was it Conroy? No, that wasn't it…close, but not quite. No, wait. It was Convy. In his mind, Jake could hear Holly talking about the creep.

Of course the program was asking for a first name, too, and an inmate number if possible. Well, he didn't have any numbers, and he suspected there couldn't be too many Convys in the system, even if he couldn't remember the guy's first name. It wasn't something he wanted to ask Holly right now. She probably wouldn't be comfortable with knowing that he wanted to track down her assailant. Jake entered his own e-mail address, name and phone number in the appropriate spots in the program, and went on to other things on his computer. With any luck the Ohio Department of Corrections would be quick, and before they left for the trial he'd have an answer.

In a few moments he was immersed in his possible testimony on Barclay. It was only when he and Holly were both in the red Escalade heading for the courthouse that he realized he'd never gotten an answer to his e-mail. By then he was focused on two things: testifying against Barclay and keeping Holly safe while he did so. They drove to the courthouse in relative peace, not seeing any dark-blue SUVs or any other vehicles that were obviously following them.

"Maybe hiding out for a week was the right thing to do after all," Holly said as they got out in the covered parking garage at the courthouse. "At least Big Red here is back in one piece and so are both of us."

She looked him up and down, and Jake felt quite complimented until he realized that she was just checking his appearance before he got into court. Still, he couldn't think of anyone else he'd rather have straighten his tie. "You'll just have to do that again once we get our coats off and go through the metal detectors," he reminded her.

"I know," she said, sounding almost a little dreamy. "But that's okay…."

Jake whistled on their way into the building. If he didn't know better, he would have said his reserved assistant was looking for reasons to touch him. Maybe there was hope for the two of them outside work yet.

Holly smoothed the skirt of her dark print dress as she sat down in the courtroom bench. The room felt charged with a quiet excitement as she surveyed all the different participants in the trial. As Rose had predicted, the jury was chosen and instructed by midmorning, and the attorneys were ready for opening statements before lunch.

The district attorney's offices had been full of potential witnesses when she and Jake had arrived. Almost all the participants were familiar faces by now. Many, in fact, were related to her. The witness list Rose and her boss had put together was starting to look like a Vance family reunion, especially now that Tricia Streeter had become Tricia Vance. The beautiful, sharp-witted air force investigator made a great addition to family gatherings, and the difference in her cousin Travis since Tricia had come on the scene was incredible. He seemed like a happy, fulfilled man again for the first time in years. Now with their mutual parts in testifying against Barclay, Holly was looking forward to seeing just what kind of teamwork Travis and his new bride were capable of.

Her uncle Max looked every inch the CIA handler he was as he stood over in the corner talking to district attorney Kirk Callahan. Meanwhile Jake chatted with her cousin Peter, the two of them looking more like best buddies than a couple of government intelligence agents pitted against a major crime boss. They looked handsome in their dark suits, and Holly thought that Alistair Barclay was going to start sweating buckets when he saw what was arrayed against him.

Now they were in the courtroom, with Jake taking his place in the front row of seats behind Rose, Kirk and the rest of the prosecutor's team. He was still next to Peter Vance, who had his father Max on the other side of him. Tricia and Travis filled out the row. Holly noticed that when Barclay looked over at the crowd behind the district attorney, there did seem to be a fine sheen of perspiration glazing his forehead, making his sparse pale-red hair appear even sparser. The handkerchief he mopped his brow with may have been fine linen, but he just didn't cut the same kind of figure in his designer suit that the witnesses against him did in their less expensive versions. Holly had to smile at that, wondering if the integrity and dignity they wore with theirs made the difference.

"I see he brought in the big guns," said the woman who slid into the bench next to Holly before the judge entered the room. "Does the man really think that having high-priced lawyers from the coast will help him?" Lidia Vance shook her head, an expression of amusement twitching across her face.

"Who's handling the lunch rush?" Holly asked, noting that her aunt was wearing a sleekly tailored pantsuit that she would never have worn to work at the café.

"Fiona and the rest of them. With all of my men here, I couldn't very well stay away, could I? Besides, in all the years we've been married, this is the first time that Max has been able to talk about what he does here in town. I wouldn't miss it for the world." Holly was about to question her aunt's statement about "all of her men" when she noticed that even her cousin Sam had slid into a seat between the prosecution and where they were sitting, making the cousin quota complete for all her male cousins.

"So where's Lucia?" She was the only one of Lidia's children not in the courtroom, which made Holly sure that her cousin must be working.

"Probably in full turnout gear someplace, or rescuing a cat up a tree," Lidia said with a twinkle in her eye. "Her shift ends tonight, though, so I suspect her to join us back here tomorrow."

"Good," Holly said. Her firefighter cousin was within months of her age, and between their demanding jobs they hadn't had time together since before Thanksgiving. The only drawback to Lucia's joining them in the courtroom would be that she'd see in an instant what Holly could hide from most of the world about her feelings for Jake. Before she could dwell on that tiny problem, the bailiff was telling them to stand while the judge entered the courtroom, and the trial began.

At first Holly felt terribly uncomfortable watching the trial proceedings. The last time she'd been in a courtroom for any length of time, it had been during Victor Convy's trial. For part of that experience, she had felt as if she'd been the one on trial herself rather than Convy. Fortunately there were enough friendly, familiar faces here that it only took a short time for her to push away the bad memories of Convy's trial and focus instead on much better thoughts.

There were so many good things to focus on during this trial. It was a great relief to think that the drug problems that Colorado Springs had seen grow and multiply during the last two years could be at an end with the breakup of the Diablo crime syndicate. Holly had seen enough at the women's shelter as she'd volunteered there to know what drugs did to a community and the families in it.

She was proud of her own family for playing such a large part in winning this particular fight. She'd spent her whole life growing up with two brothers and more boy cousins than girls, with Lucia and her playing a lot more football and soccer than the boys ever joined them in any quieter games. Now to see the same guys she'd squabbled with in loving companionship actually changing their corner of the world made her heart swell. Jake looked like he belonged up there in the ranks of the heroes. In line with Uncle Max, Peter and Travis, he didn't seem to be the society playboy she would have considered him even a few short weeks ago.

In comparison with the Vance and Montgomery families in the row behind the prosecution, the defense lineup looked pretty pathetic. Two men Holly suspected were Barclay's construction foremen looked uncomfortable in the second row back, while three young women in too tight clothing had separated themselves as far as possible from each other in the rows behind Barclay. Otherwise there didn't appear to be much in the way of a defense presence besides the hotel magnate's legal team.

Quite a few journalists filled up the back half of Barclay's side of the gallery, and Holly noted Colleen Montgomery among the *Sentinel*'s reporters and their sketch artist, and two local radio and television reporters she recognized from FBI press conferences in the past. Back behind some of the journalists, a handsome man in a dark suit caught her eye. She wasn't sure, but it looked like Lidia's nephew Alessandro Donato.

The judge had forbidden cameras during the trial, which was normal, and there were no recording devices except those used by the court clerk, so Holly watched most of the reporters writing feverishly while Barclay's lead defense attorney made his opening statement explaining the "grave errors" that had been committed in this wrongful prosecution of his client.

Holly wasn't sure anybody was buying his speech.

If Barclay was trying to look innocent, he was failing in her estimation. Apparently he wasn't doing well in Lidia's eyes either, as Holly caught snatches of muttering under her aunt's breath in Italian, which she hardly ever used unless she was saying something less than kind that she didn't want those around her to understand.

During the lunch break that followed the opening statements, Holly was surprised to see that instead of discussing the trial at length, Jake and her cousins seemed focused on the college football bowl games going on during the week. Even that bantering quieted down for a few minutes when Barclay's defense team walked into the same restaurant they had chosen. "Tomorrow, we go to the café," Lidia declared. "I know it's farther away, but I'll make sure from now on, as long as the trial lasts, that we have the side room cleared for any of you who want to use it."

"I appreciate it, Mrs. Vance," the district attorney said, "and I'll take you up on it as long as you won't try to feed us for free. I know you already feed half of the Colorado Springs police force without letting them pay full price—"

"Half? All," Lidia said. "No one who works with Sam is allowed to pay like another customer while I'm cooking at the café. Their jobs are too dangerous."

Sam, arriving at the table late after what Holly suspected was a call in to check the status of his current cases at work, stopped behind his mother and leaned his chin down on her head as he hugged her from behind. "Mom, your job at that big restaurant stove is probably as dangerous as most of ours. But we appreciate it all, really. I'm with Kirk, though. Let him pay for lunch…maybe he can find a way to put it on Barclay's legal bill." The laughter that followed broke up any other conversations at the table for a while, and Holly spent the rest of the lunch hour trying to dispel her feelings that she was just at another family reunion.

It was a hard notion to shake even when they were all back in the courtroom. Her uncle Max was the first witness called and Holly wasn't sure what was more fascinating, hearing his testimony about his part in linking Barclay to La Mano Oscura, or watching Aunt Lidia hear his testimony beside her. Her chest swelled with pride as he outlined his part in the plan to take down the drug ring. More than once she pressed a hand to her chest, murmuring in surprise about something he'd said. And Lidia's smile of triumph when Barclay's lawyers couldn't win any points against him was positively beatific.

Things got even more dramatic when Peter took the stand late in the afternoon. His testimony provided a clear chain of evidence for the files taken from Baltasar Escalante's computer, some of which Holly knew mentioned Barclay directly. Then it was her turn to press a hand to her chest in surprise when Barclay's attorney cross-examined her handsome cousin.

"How do you know that the evidence you say you provided wasn't compromised by the various hand-offs made between this Escalante and the FBI?" the defense attorney asked, a sneer on his face.

"Because there weren't any hand-offs," Peter said. "I downloaded the files from Escalante's hard drive myself, and put them directly into the hands of Special Agent Montgomery in Venezuela."

The lawyer's expression changed to one of dismay, and he stumbled onto a totally different line of questioning that didn't seem to lead anywhere. He gave up after a few minutes and Peter left the stand while Holly was still trying to breathe. Jake had been on the multiagency raid in Venezuela that they'd all talked about? She knew he'd been out of the office in November but he had just called his trip "routine business, nothing to worry about" in his typical understated fashion. She made a mental note to ask him about his idea of routine business when they next got together outside the courtroom.

She looked at her watch once Peter left the stand, and saw that it was past four-thirty in the afternoon. It came as no surprise when the judge called a halt to the proceedings for the day, and told everyone assembled that they'd start again at nine the next morning.

"Come on, I'll take you back to your car," Jake said once they left the courtroom. They took the stairs to avoid the masses at the elevators and beat most of the trial participants to the courthouse garage.

"I'm tempted to follow you home," Jake said once he'd helped her inside the Escalade. "I hate to think of you alone in case Barclay's goon latches on to us again."

Holly shook her head. "It's not going to happen, Jake. Not tonight. I should be much more worried about you, right before your testimony. Maybe I should follow you home instead."

"Yeah, well, you can follow me back here to Rose's office then, because I think we're sending out for Chinese and going over testimony for a few hours," he said. "Do you want to call her on my cell phone and tell her to send in another order of kung pao chicken?"

Holly knew it was strictly business, but it was hard for the reality of Jake and Rose, together for hours over takeout food, not to worry her at all. Jake was such a charmer that it was difficult to think he wouldn't turn some of that savoir faire on for Rose without even meaning to. She'd watched him before, seeing charisma just ooze out of his pores simply because he was talking to a beautiful woman. "No thanks, count me out," she said, even though she wanted to say something totally different. This was something she had to face if there was any chance of having a relationship of any kind with Jake. And now was as good a time as any to face it. "You two have plenty to go over and I'd just be in the way." Jake didn't push the issue any further, and he let her get into her Jeep without argument in their parking garage.

He followed her as far as their routes would allow, then Holly turned toward home, and she could see him waving in her rearview mirror. If her mother noticed that she was more quiet than usual that night, she didn't say anything.

Coming into the courtroom, Holly felt strangely out of touch with Jake for the first time in weeks. They hadn't ridden in together and she was surprised at how much she missed that. "How was your trip over here?" he asked the moment he saw her.

"Fine, and uneventful," she said, reaching out to straighten his tie a little. His suit was even nicer than yesterday's, and she noticed that the tie she straightened was the red one with dark-blue stripes that he wore virtually every time he went to court for Bureau things. Athletes had their lucky socks, and FBI agents had lucky ties, Holly decided. "Good luck up there." She inclined her head toward the front of the courtroom.

"Thanks. You're staying to watch, aren't you?"

"I wouldn't be anyplace else. Is your family coming?"

Jake shook his head. "My parents will stay as far away as possible from this trial, since the man is technically still my father's opponent in the mayoral race. Until he's convicted, anyway. Until then, my father doesn't want any hint of impropriety. I expect the defense attorney to bring up my family, just as a way of muddying the waters."

"Maybe he'll be so busy trying to break your testimony that he won't have time to do that," Holly said.

"Gee, great news either way, huh?" Jake's grin was rueful. "Well, get to your seat. It looks like we're about to start."

Holly thought she might know a little bit about how Lidia had felt the day before. Now it was her turn to feel nervous and proud at the same time because someone she cared so much for was up on the witness stand. Jake and Rose had obviously gone over things for a long time last night. They kept a polished, professional demeanor and everything flowed smoothly.

She risked a glance at Barclay more than once. If Max and Peter's testimony had made him sweat the day before, this appeared to make him even more uncomfortable as Jake's testimony went on. At first Barclay looked confident, but his smile slipped, and then disappeared altogether when Rose had Jake explain the layers of passwords that he'd decoded, which broke into Barclay's secret files that matched Escalante's.

The exhibits Rose entered into the court record were large and thorough. Jake explained the printouts in detail as each page went up on a screen the entire courtroom could see. The evidence was plain. In the deepest layers of files Jake had untangled from layers of encryption, there were neat rows of figures, and lists of dates and payments for distributions of narcotics.

Barclay's attorney seemed to be at a loss when he sprang up to cross-examine Jake. He stood in what looked like a thoughtful pose, done by a very good actor, next to the defense table. "Have you ever considered, Agent Montgomery, that Mr. Barclay had discovered that one of his employees was actually in league with this ring, and was trying to build enough evidence to come to the authorities?"

"No, I hadn't," Jake fired back. "Because if anyone was doing that, they apparently were distributing their ill-gotten gains in Mr. Barclay's own account in the Cayman Islands, which is what that last column of figures refers to in the table that's still up on the projector." There was soft laughter from several areas of the courtroom.

"Isn't it true that your father is the mayor of Colorado Springs?" the lawyer asked, and Jake agreed with him.

"And isn't it true that Mr. Barclay has announced his intention to run against him?"

"To the best of my knowledge," Jake answered, looking a little more grim now.

"But if you, the mayor's son, help convict Mr. Barclay on these trumped-up charges, the campaign will be over, correct?" Holly found herself disliking this man incredibly. She knew it was his job to cast doubt on Jake's testimony any way that he could, and the more rational part of her mind told her she ought to be happy that this was the worst he could do.

"If Barclay's convicted, he won't be running for mayor." Jake's refusal to make a simple answer to the question pointed out more than the lawyer wanted, Holly knew.

At that moment Jake caught her eye, and held her gaze as the disgruntled lawyer muttered "No further questions" and let Jake leave the stand. The wink he gave her communicated volumes. Holly was amazed at how much passed between them in that one look, which seemed to be Jake's way of saying "Hey, we did it, and it could have been a lot worse," all in one small gesture. She knew her smile back at him was broad, and she hoped it conveyed what she felt in her heart for this man just at this moment.

Chapter Ten

"You were fantastic," Rose D'Arcy called when Jake came into the side room at the Stagecoach Café.

"Well, you weren't too bad yourself," Jake countered. It had been fun and challenging to work with a prosecutor he actually knew for a change. In most of his FBI testimony, he'd ended up knowing the person he was testifying against more thoroughly than the legal team who asked for his services. It was one of the hazards of delving into someone's personal files to extract information from them. "It was great to work with somebody I knew was good coming in."

"Thanks. I appreciate the compliment. Now if all this expertise actually gets us somewhere…" Rose looked around the restaurant. "Who else is coming for lunch? Didn't Holly come with you?"

"She's coming. Her cousin Lucia was there today, and they wanted to ride over together."

"And talk about you," Rose said with a grin.

"Yeah, probably." When admitting that about most women, Jake would have felt silly, but with Holly he actually wanted to know what she and her cousin would say. He was a little anxious about seeing her when she came into the café.

Having Rose here without Holly, and without the rest of the team, gave him an opportunity, though. "There is one small legal favor I wouldn't mind having from you," he said, trying to sound casual. "There's a set of records I want to check on in the Ohio correctional system, and I'm having a little trouble accessing them."

"Holly told you." Rose's voice was flat, and her eyes narrowed.

"She did. And I want to do all that I can to make sure her assailant stays in a place where he can't hurt anybody again."

"Sounds like a great idea to me. If I had already passed the bar five years ago I would have offered my services for free to put Victor Convy away."

Victor Convy. Jake burned the name into his memory this time. "I agree. You use your resources when you go back to the office, and I'll use mine, and we'll try to track this guy down and make sure he stays put."

"Happily. Now, moving on to a much pleasanter

subject, we're about to be joined by the rest of the crew," Rose said. The district attorney and one of his other assistants came into the room at the same time Holly and Lucia joined them in the doorway. Looking at Holly, Jake felt more relieved than he could imagine that this trial was almost over and they could move on with their lives.

When Holly got closer to him, Jake noticed that she looked a little troubled about something. "What were you and Rose talking about?" she asked.

Now he felt stuck. He couldn't very well say "nothing" because she'd know it wasn't the truth. But he didn't feel like telling her what they'd been discussing, either.

"Trial stuff," Rose said smoothly, coming up between them. "And Lucia's mom says to sit down at the table before things get cold."

The gorgeous, dark-haired young woman that Jake figured must be Holly's cousin Lucia laughed. "Great. Your first day as a group here and she's got lunch fixed for you when you come in. You must rate. Usually she lets my firefighters, or Sam's police friends, order off the menu at least once before she starts cooking special stuff."

"I think it's the family special," her brother Travis piped up, moving in to join the group as well. "There's so many of us here, Mom probably put together Thanksgiving dinner, only without the turkey."

Jake wondered what else was left and was about to open his mouth to ask when Lidia herself breezed into the room, urging everyone to sit down. In a moment platters of salad, pans of lasagna, huge baskets of rolls and mountains of other delights filled the table and were being passed from person to person. Somehow he'd ended up between Holly and Lucia, who were both enthusiastically filling their plates for lunch.

Jake figured he must have looked stunned by the quantity of food, and the volume of people around the table. "Poor Jake," Holly said, passing a basket of rolls. "You never had any Italian family dinners. I'll bet with a name like Montgomery, big family gatherings were almost sedate compared to this."

"A little quieter," he agreed. "Unless we're talking holidays at Aunt Fiona's. Then this noise level is just about right, and while the type of food on the table might be different, the amount here matches hers."

He looked down the way at Travis, who was dishing out a square of lasagna. "Man, I'm glad it's you testifying this afternoon and not me. If I had to get up on the stand after this I'd be fighting the urge to nap."

Travis smiled, waving in dismissal. "Not a problem. I'm just wondering what's for dessert. Did Mom do deep dish apple pie or cannoli?"

Lucia laughed beside Jake. "Oh, come on, she knew you and Dad and Sam were all going to be eating this lunch. What do you think?"

Jake resisted the urge to groan when Travis and his sister answered together, "Both!"

After that lunch, Holly did find it a little more difficult to stay awake in the courtroom that afternoon. Aunt Lidia's cooking was the best ever, and she'd missed having the chance at any holiday dinners with that part of the family, so today had been a welcome change of pace. Still, she wondered what Rose and Jake had really been discussing so seriously when she and Lucia entered the side room of the café. Jake's testimony was finished; what kind of "trial stuff" did they have to go over?

She chided herself for even worrying for a moment about Jake and her own cousin. If she was ever going to have anything serious and lasting with Jake, she was going to have to trust him. It was difficult for her to trust people, even this long after the incident with Victor Convy. But surely this was connected to her trust in God. She'd put her trust in Him for so long; if Jake truly was the right person for her, the Lord would lead them both to the right decision.

Holly was pulled from her serious thoughts of the future with Jake by the court bailiff calling for Major Patricia Vance. It was still difficult for her to connect that formal address with her new cousin Tricia. She looked very professional in her Air Force dress uniform, and Holly was buoyed by the look that passed between her and her new husband Travis before she testified. It was good to see Travis so obviously and deeply in love after the hard times he'd had.

Rose's boss, Kirk, was back asking Tricia questions now. When she was finished with her testimony, there was little doubt of the connection between La Mano Oscura and the organization's drug traffic from Venezuela, and Alistair Barclay. He was just connected in too many ways through the things that Tricia had uncovered by investigating General George Hadley. Barclay's lawyer worked on the finer points of her investigation and the things that tied it the most incriminatingly to his client, but it all held fast. Tricia left the stand smiling.

She was followed by Travis, who solidified the connection between the general and Barclay even more. The only chink the defense could find in his armor was a pretty weak one. The lawyer got him to admit that yes, Max Vance was his father, and his brother Peter was the CIA agent who'd uncovered Baltasar Escalante's identity as the head of the drug ring, and his alleged ties to Barclay. "And the lady who just testified, Major Vance. What a coincidence, she's another Vance. What relation would she be to you?"

"She is my wife," Travis said, pride and happiness the only things evident in his voice as he answered with a smile.

"Your family seems to have a personal vendetta

against my client," the lawyer said, as Rose and Kirk quickly objected. While they aired their objections to the judge, who ordered the offending comment stricken from the record, Holly looked over at Alistair Barclay. He looked even less confident than he had earlier in the trial, and he seemed to have aged in two days.

When the argument was over Kirk went back to ask Travis a few more questions, centering on his relationship with Tricia before their marriage. His testimony was a reminder of how much the couple had gone through, having been college sweethearts over a decade before. Travis didn't waver while Kirk had him tell of his marriage to Allison, and the horrible accident that took her life as well as that of their young daughter. "So you had an opinion on how to proceed when Major Streeter came back into your life?" Kirk asked.

Travis nodded. "With my experiences I know that life is precious, unlike the drug dealers who've infested our city lately. And I decided quickly that if I was to be blessed with a second chance at happiness, I'd take it. Quickly."

Holly had a lump in her throat that felt the size of a grapefruit. *What a testimony to love,* she thought. But definitely something she never wanted to have to go through on a witness stand. It intensified her desire to finish this chapter of her life, as Jake's assistant, before they started a new chapter that might include a serious relationship. How she would manage things, she didn't know, but it had to be done.

While she sat trying to puzzle out just when and how to act, Kirk asked the judge to call a slightly early end to trial proceedings for the day. "We call as our next witness former General George Hadley, your honor," the district attorney said. "And due to the security level we need to maintain while he's in the courtroom, and the probable length of the testimony, we request that we be allowed to call him starting tomorrow morning."

"Very well," the judge said. "Trial to resume at 10:00 a.m. tomorrow." There was a general murmur through the courtroom with the stir of people getting ready to leave. Holly happened to look back at Barclay. He was pale to the point of being pasty, and gripped the edge of the table like a life raft.

That picture was still with Holly the next morning when her cell phone rang as she was getting ready to go into work. "Come straight to court," Rose told her. "You guys have to be here right at ten when they start proceedings." It was all that she'd say, making Holly wonder what on earth was going to happen.

Jake, when she found him shortly after they'd both gone through the courthouse metal detectors, was as clueless as she was. "I have some ideas, all of which would be good news for our side," he said.

"But concrete evidence of what's going to happen when we walk in there? Nothing except Rose's phone call this morning. I take it she called you, too."

"With the same message, to get here on time and see what happens." Rose and Kirk had obviously been busy making phone calls, because by the time Holly and Jake had picked up a cup of coffee at the ground floor stand in the courthouse, and taken the elevator to the second floor courtroom where Barclay's trial was going on, there were quite a few people they knew standing and sitting in the gallery. The only ones missing were Rose and Kirk, and Barclay and his defense team.

A few minutes later, the jury had all filed in to their seats, and the court officials were in place as well. When the attorneys came out of the judge's chambers and took their places, Jake and Holly exchanged glances. "You've attended a whole lot more trials than I have," Holly said to him. "Tell me if that was as significant as it looked to me."

Barclay was ushered in from a side room somewhere, and the bailiff was calling the proceedings to order before Jake could answer. He didn't get the opportunity to say anything before the judge answered Holly's questions for her by turning to the jury and beginning a speech.

"Ladies and gentlemen of the jury, I want to thank you for your participation in the due process of law in El Paso County, and I want to tell you that your services will no longer be needed. Mr. Barclay's attorneys have advised me that he wishes to change his plea to guilty on the charges before him and as such, this trial is adjourned."

Rose and Kirk were smiling broadly, while Barclay's lawyers glowered. He himself looked relieved, and the noise level in the courtroom rose in a very short time.

"For somebody who hasn't seen many of these, you caught on quickly," Jake told Holly.

"Well, from my limited experience, I knew that having the lawyers talk to the judge right before the beginning of the day's trial wasn't quite normal. Plus yesterday they said there would be extra security for General Hadley…I guess that's just plain old Mr. Hadley now, isn't it? And no one in the way of extra security was here, and neither was he."

"Very good, Watson," Jake said with a grin. "In any case, it means we're out of here. Done. We won't be ringing in the new year waiting for this whole mess to be over with."

"You've got that right," Rose said, beaming while she clapped them both on the shoulder. "This is excellent, better than we could have hoped for. And if Barclay's lawyers are to be believed, you're half of what made him decide to call it a day."

"Really? I just figured he had no desire to let a

jury hear what Hadley would say against him," Jake said.

"Like I said, you're half of it. Apparently nobody on the other side expected you to come up with nearly as much of his private information as you did. That, combined with Hadley's testimony, was going to sink Barclay once and for all. If he plea bargains now, he might possibly see a few of his golden years on the outside. At the very least, he'll be in a better class of institution."

"I'm not sure he deserves any consideration, but I'm glad for your sake and for ours that this trial is over. Guess you have to go through the sentencing phase yet." Jake looked up at the front of the courtroom.

Rose nodded. "We do, but that will be a few days at least. For now Kirk will probably want to celebrate with everyone to blow off a little steam first."

"Sounds good to me. We definitely have some celebrating to do." Jake's pointed look in her direction made Holly shiver with anticipation.

Jake looked around him in the private dining room, wondering how even D.A. Kirk Callahan could have gotten this room at the Cliff House Restaurant at such short notice. Surely even on a Wednesday, in the week between Christmas and New Year's Eve, it would have been difficult. After all the hours he'd personally put in, though, he wasn't about to turn down a celebration of this magnitude. It was especially great because he had so much, personally, to celebrate.

Kirk came in, introducing Jake to his wife. She was a pretty blond woman who appeared to be as happy as her husband that this trial was almost over. "I'm sure you're looking forward to seeing a great deal more of him."

"Definitely. Just seeing any of him at all will be a new and different thing. Christmas was the only day he's taken off in a month, and even then once he sat down to play Billy's new video game with him, he fell asleep with the controller in his hand." Still, she smiled indulgently at her husband.

As several of the others involved in the trial filtered in and began to find seats at the long table, Jake started to wonder if it had been such a great idea to let Rose talk him into letting her bring Holly this evening. He had so much to discuss with Holly that he would have rather brought her himself. And the two women still weren't here. Several other members of the Vance family had come in, making an impressive array around the table.

Everywhere he looked, Jake saw couples. Maybe there had always been this many of them around him, and he just hadn't noticed because he wasn't all that interested. But now that he planned to ask Holly to start seeing him in a serious way, everyone seemed to be paired. Max and Lidia Vance looked more like newlyweds than the actual newlyweds among their offspring did, if that was possible.

Musing over that while standing near the table, Jake almost jumped when there was suddenly a hand on his back and a low voice in his ear. "You look deep in thought," Holly said as he tried not to upset his lime and tonic water.

"Just got to daydreaming while waiting for you two to show up," he said, enjoying the two beautiful women beside him. Rose had changed out of the more severe suit she'd worn in court into a black ensemble offset with sparkling earrings. Holly, ever more sedate, still wore her dark-brown hair pulled back in her normal French braid, and a black pantsuit less flashy than her cousin's, but every bit as elegant. "You look very nice. Definitely worth the wait."

"I should hope so. We're not even the last ones to show up," Holly said, motioning him toward the table. "My mother told me to blame her for our tardy appearance anyway. She and Rose started talking when she came in to pick me up."

"We made a lunch date for next week. I can hardly wait to catch up on all the missed holiday activities, now that I'm free again." Rose started toward the table. "But for tonight I've got to help Kirk host all this, so I'll catch you later, all right? And both of you, order steak or lobster or something, because you deserve it."

Shortly after that the party got going, and in the chatter, ordering appetizers and dinner and talking with everyone else around him, Jake didn't get a chance at more than pleasantries with Holly for another hour.

"Is there a possibility that I can take you home instead of letting Rose do it?" he asked during a quieter moment as the waiters cleared salads.

"I suppose. Do you think we can stop worrying about whoever was following us now?" Holly looked more concerned than Jake expected her to, but he reminded himself that she and her mother were basically alone in their home without much protection. He thought about suggesting that she call Mike and ask if King could spend a week or so at the house, but it wouldn't be fair to the big dog to be alone all day, and he certainly didn't want that big furry lug in the office.

"We should be all right. Neither of us has seen anything since we came back to town, right?" Holly's nod was confirmation to his question. "And I think that now that Barclay's entered a plea, it would make little sense to threaten me any more."

"Then if you want to take me home, that will be all right. It will be good to get back to something like a normal routine tomorrow. I've honestly forgotten what that is like."

"Judging from the conversation around the table,

you're in good company," Jake said. Before he could tell Holly that he was anxious to get back to the office just so that things could be different, Kirk called from across the table to ask a question, then the entrees were served, and the night passed all too quickly in similar fashion, without another chance to talk about the future.

By the time dessert and coffee rolled around, Jake noticed that several of the couples and groups at the table were making their goodbyes. Travis and Tricia Vance left first, and several other twos and threes were quick to follow. In a few minutes it was mostly Kirk and his wife, and Rose and others from the district attorney's staff. "Well, why don't we leave these folks to settle up the bill so that they can go home, too," Jake said.

"I'll tell Rose what we agreed on and meet you in a moment." Holly got up and went to talk to her cousin. Jake pondered how to do things now. He didn't want to bring up the subject in a setting as unromantic as his vehicle. For this conversation he wanted to be face-to-face with Holly, with no other distractions so that he could hear what she had to say, and see her expression.

Around Holly, though, he still felt awkward in so many situations. She meant so much more to him than just being his assistant now, and they'd shared so much in that cabin. Even though his brain was screaming that he should detour, find a quiet place in the lobby or go someplace for another cup of coffee, or anything just to talk to her, Jake found himself at the car all too quickly. He helped Holly up into the high seat and closed her door. It was far too cold to sit and talk in the vehicle, so he started the engine and got the heater going while he drove the much too short distance to her home.

"Would you like to come in for a minute?" Jake wasn't sure if the hopeful tone in her voice was because Holly wanted him there, or wished he would leave quickly. He decided to stop second-guessing her and agreed to go inside.

The front room was dark except for the lights on the Christmas tree, and wherever Marilyn Vance was, she didn't come to the front of the house to say hello right away. Jake found himself hoping that she'd gone to bed early so that he could have a quiet conversation with her daughter, hopefully the first of many in this cozy front room.

"About getting back to normal tomorrow," Holly began as she sat on the other end of the sofa from where he sat. She smoothed invisible wrinkles out of her slacks with nervous hands, and Jake's heart sank. "I think we need to talk about that."

"I guess we do. I'd really hoped that things wouldn't be so normal. I've been waiting for this trial to be over, Holly, so that we could get back to the office. But I don't want to fall back into our old routines. I've seen you in a whole different light during the course of this trial, and I want to see more of that person." Jake felt more nervous than he'd been in years.

"I want to see more of *you,* Holly, and I'm not talking about just working with you. I'd like to start seeing each other outside of work, and soon. Could we go out tomorrow night? We could make it low-key, a movie or something, but—"

Holly sighed. "No, Jake. Please, I'm just not ready."

He reached for her hand, but Holly moved as far from him as she could on the couch. "Is there anything I can say, or do, to convince you otherwise?" He couldn't think of anything to say, really, but he wanted this to happen so much.

"Not yet. It…doesn't feel right, not tomorrow. I'm just not ready," she repeated, looking down at the carpet, a troubled expression on her face.

"Well, how long then? Another couple days? A week? What will it take for you to be ready?" Even though Jake wanted to be patient and understanding, this wasn't the way he was used to conversations with women going. He had no idea what happened next in a situation like this one, so different from his previous encounters, and so far out of his control.

"I don't know. I can't tell you tonight. I can only ask you to give me more time."

"If that's what you want." Jake rose, at a loss for anything else to say. "I guess I better leave now. See you in the morning?"

"Of course. Be careful driving home," Holly said, walking him to the door.

As if that matters, Jake felt like saying, but he left silently instead. The joyful Christmas carols that came on the radio when he started the engine seemed like an invasion. "Peace on earth? This is not my idea of peace," he grumbled under his breath to God, if He was listening. In a swift movement, he switched off the radio so that he could drive home in stony, brooding silence to match his mood.

Chapter Eleven

Thursday morning, Holly had to force herself to go into work and face Jake. Once she got there she was sorry she'd made the effort, as instead of Jake being there, all she found was a message on her voice mail. "I'm taking the morning as a personal holiday to try to get things in order here. I probably have enough to do to spend the entire day working from home. I'll call in later," his message said in a voice devoid of any emotion.

"Great. All that stress for nothing," Holly told the phone, aware that it wouldn't answer her back. Still, she couldn't blame Jake for shutting her out. She hadn't been encouraging last night. Her feelings right now were so mixed up, and she wasn't sure how to go about sorting them out.

While she sat at her computer and tried to work

through the mail that had accumulated in the week they'd been paying more attention to the trial than to work, she talked to God in a way that was more matter-of-fact than her most usual prayer. "Okay, I need help here," Holly said softly. There wasn't anybody to overhear her and worry about her sanity, so she had the conversation out loud. "I really don't know what to do about everything, Lord. If Jake and I are supposed to be together, then several things have to change. Who do I talk to about this, where do I go?"

Before she had finished with the pile of mail and messages on the desk, the phone rang. When Holly answered it, Rose was on the other end. "So, what's up? I didn't get a chance to catch up with you after dinner last night because we were so busy with the details. Do you want to meet me at the Stagecoach for lunch?"

Holly knew God was good, but this was incredible, and it made her grin. "Sure," she told her cousin. "That might be just what I need."

Of course the restaurant was busy, between the regulars who hadn't taken the week between the holidays off, and all the folks who were on vacation of some kind and decided to spend a day downtown in Colorado Springs. Still, she and Rose were led to a more remote booth without too long a wait. Once they'd ordered, Rose leaned over the table, absently playing with the straw in her diet cola. "Okay, so what was going on last night? Why did Jake take you home? Are you still being followed, or was it just concern?"

"Neither of those, actually." Now that she had the opportunity to talk about all this with someone who might understand, Holly found herself tongue-tied.

This time, Rose's nature as a good attorney and nosy cousin helped Holly. She didn't let the silence last long. "Oh? So what else is there? Did he offer you a healthy bonus as a reward for all your help during the trial? Or is there more to his appreciation of you than just liking your work? Maybe I'm off base, but I'd say by looking at the two of you, that something besides work went on at the ranch."

"A lot went on, and it has me feeling really confused," Holly told her. "I've thought that I was in love with Jake for a long time, but I didn't expect anything to actually happen with my feelings, because I didn't think either of us would ever change enough for me to act on my feelings."

The server came with their lunch, and Rose looked like she was going to burst waiting for the woman to put the food on the table and leave. "So what happened? And what do you mean by saying you thought you were in love with him?"

"Man, you're good. You just don't miss anything. Do you ever lose any cases?" Rose was making her smile when she'd felt like crying so recently.

"All too often, but that's part of the game. And don't try to weasel out of answering me." Rose waved a bread stick at her.

"Okay. Before, I thought I was in love with Jake, but in the last few weeks, I really fell in love with him, and the feelings are different. They're deeper, but I feel so much more vulnerable. It's making me very protective, not just of me but of him, too, and I don't want anything to happen to jeopardize that."

"And how does he feel?"

Holly sighed. "He asked me last night to start seeing him outside of work, and I believe that he's serious."

"You sound like there's a but there."

"Several. I'm not quite ready for that yet. And he got pretty aggravated when I told him that I couldn't do that on his timetable."

"He knows about your past, and he seems pretty accepting of it," Rose said, startling Holly a little.

It was definitely a statement by her cousin, not a question, which surprised her. "Has he actually said something like that to you?"

Rose shook her head. "No. He's gone out of his way to communicate that he knows about Convy and everything that happened, without discussing it with me in any way that would violate your privacy. But if you have any doubts about his feelings for you, I'm a pretty good judge of those things, and I'd say they're sincere."

"Thanks. That's a big comfort." Something dawned on her as she sat at the table. "That's what you two were talking about here before lunch the other day, wasn't it?" She buried her face in her hands. "Oh, no. And to think I was worried because I was afraid he was flirting with you."

"Sorry, no such thing. He only has eyes for you right now, which is incredible. The old Jake Montgomery would have charmed me out of my socks while we worked together all those hours, but it certainly didn't happen this time." Rose put down her fork. "If it were anybody less deserving than you that he was hooked on, I'd complain. I miss the old Jake. He was fun."

"For other people. It was less fun thinking I was in love with him and watching him flirt with every attractive woman in sight."

"I imagine. So if you're not worried about his feelings, and you're pretty sure of your own, what do you do now?"

"That's the hard part." Holly sighed, looking at her half-eaten salad. "I have to find a way to separate our work relationship and our personal relationship. Then I'll be ready to actually date him, I think."

Rose shrugged. "I'd think that would be the easy part. Isn't there anybody else in your office that would switch places with you? For the short term it would solve the problem. If Jake didn't agree to the switch, he could always ask you to help find him a new assistant."

"That is one possibility," Holly said. "And you're right, that would solve the problem in the short run. Thanks, Rose. Now, do you have any problems you want to unload on me in return?"

"Personal problems? Don't I wish?" Her cousin rolled her eyes. "This job has me so busy I don't have enough social life to come up with problems. Maybe that's my New Year's resolution, to get a life."

Holly lifted her iced tea in a toast. "I'll agree to that one." Her appetite renewed, she went back to the salad. With Rose's suggestion in her mind, suddenly the café's dessert cart sounded tempting.

The half-day rest hadn't helped put Jake in a better mood. He rode the elevator up to the FBI offices, looking at his reflection in the polished steel sides of the car. He didn't look as bad as he felt. It shouldn't be too hard to put on a brave face and pretend that he was doing just fine for Holly. The doors opened and he went down the hall and through the door of the resident agency. It was largely deserted. About half the personnel seemed to be using the last few days of the year to take leave and stay home with their families.

The door to Holly's outer office was closed and he stood before it for a minute, took a deep breath and walked into an empty room. So much for his brave front. There wasn't even a note on the desk saying where she was. Maybe when he called in earlier and copped out, she went home.

He went into his own office, where piles of mail and stacks of messages sat neatly on the desk. So Holly had spent at least some time in the office being her normal efficient self before she went home, or wherever she'd gone. It aggravated him a bit that she hadn't left any indication of where she'd gone. What if Barclay's henchman was still out there? Or what if it was someone from Escalante's organization?

Of course if he thought fairly, he hadn't given her any reason to stick around today. It would have been so much better if he'd just called her last night after leaving her house, or this morning before she left for work, or tried again here to tell her how he felt. He was frustrated that he couldn't just start some kind of whirlwind courtship now that all the barriers of the trial were gone. Several times in the last few weeks he'd thought that was what she wanted. Now she was pulling back again and he had no idea how to make things right between them.

Pushing aside his aggravation, he looked at the piles of work on his desk and decided to take out his frustration on all the junk he needed to sort through. Maybe he wouldn't feel better about his entire life in an hour, but he'd clear this pile off the desk, anyway. That had to count for something.

An hour later, the pile was mostly diminished. Of course now there was a stack nearly as high as the first one had been of documents with sticky notes attached to them, telling Holly how to deal with the things that needed to be done. And she still wasn't back in the office. Jake put the stack in the middle of her desk where she couldn't miss it, and decided to go down the hallway looking for company, or information. Surely somebody else knew where his assistant had gotten to.

In the second office he checked, he found both company and information. "She and Sara Phelps went out for coffee," Bob told him. The other special agent professed to be on his way out of the building himself. "Since there wasn't much for Sara to do around here, and both of you missed the Christmas party, I figured they could spend the afternoon visiting if they wanted."

Jake agreed. There was no reason Holly couldn't do exactly as she liked with her time. Why did it bother him so that she hadn't told him what she was doing? He thanked Bob for his help and was about to leave when the man called him back. "I keep forgetting to ask you something. Did you borrow my computer a couple weeks ago?"

"Well, yeah," Jake admitted, steeling himself for

what he expected to come next. He had hoped he wouldn't have to admit to taking the machine apart, but he wasn't about to lie to the man either. *How do I handle this one, Lord?* He really knew without an answer that the way to handle this was truthfully, making whatever apology he needed to.

"Thanks. I don't know how you had time in the middle of this case to take a look at it, or what you did to it, but the problem I'd been having with it is gone. That funny whirring noise I told Holly about cleared up, and the software glitch I hadn't even mentioned vanished, too."

"You're welcome. It actually helped me out as well on something I needed to figure out on the case, so we're both ahead this time." Jake cracked a grin for the first time in hours. Bob headed for the elevator and Jake went back to his office. Holly had told him over and over that faith was the answer to most of life's problems. Why had it taken so long for him to believe it?

Sitting in the quiet of his office, he pondered over the biggest problem in his life, and mulled over what God would want him to do about it. Just as the little problem with Bob had a simple answer, this one had one as well. It wasn't one he liked, but the moment it came to him, Jake knew it was right. Bowing his head right there, he started talking to the Lord.

"Father, You know how I feel about Holly, and how I want this relationship I believe we're supposed to have to move forward, and fast. I've never felt this way about a woman before, and it's something new for me. But I know that things have to proceed in Your time, not mine. Help me to find peace with that, and to give Holly the space she needs so that our love can grow, if that's what You have in mind for us." It was the hardest prayer he'd prayed so far, but it felt the most right. Leaning back in his chair, Jake felt an incredible sense of peace.

A few minutes later he realized with a start that he'd actually dozed off there, once he heard voices in the outer office. Getting up and going to the doorway, he saw Holly and Sara standing in front of the desk talking. They broke off their conversation when they saw him.

"Hi, Mr. Montgomery," Sara said. She smiled at him and tilted her head, making the large, dangly earrings she wore jingle slightly with the tiny bells hanging from them. "Merry Christmas. I didn't get to tell you that last week. And Happy New Year in case I don't see you tomorrow."

"The same to you, Sara. Have you had a nice holiday season so far?" Jake looked at the girl, knowing that he'd once found her attractive in her own spacey way. Now he wondered how he could have ever felt that way. She was certainly nice enough, but standing next to Holly she just didn't compare. Nobody did these days, he decided.

"Yeah, I have," Sara said. "Thank you for asking."

"Do you need me right away?" Holly asked. "If so, I can finish the conversation I was having with Sara later."

Jake needed her all right, but in his newfound peace, nothing was urgent. "Take your time," he said with a smile, trying to reassure her. "Should I make us a fresh pot of coffee, or are you done for the day?"

"I could stick around for another cup once I walk Sara down the hall," Holly told him, looking intrigued by either his question or his attitude.

"Go ahead," he said, going over and getting the coffeepot. He could hear the two of them giggling slightly as they moved away and he wondered what that was about. Then he got preoccupied with the routine of making coffee. By the time Holly came back a few minutes later, he'd poured himself a cup and was waiting for her.

"I thought we could move into my office for a few minutes," he told her. When she nodded, he poured her coffee and set it on the corner of his desk where she sat in the visitor's chair.

"Okay, what's up here? On the phone this morning you sounded the way I expected you to, unhappy and short with me. Now you're at ease. What's going on, Jake?"

He was actually smiling through this conversation. Jake was amazed. "What's going on is that I seem to be a slow learner in the faith department. A little while ago I did what I should have done before speaking to you last night, and gave the burden of our situation over to God. I'm sorry I wasn't happy with your answer last night, Holly, and even sorrier that I let it show so badly. Whatever time you need to be ready to change our relationship, you take."

Holly's eyes had widened until they were dark-brown pools during his speech. He was thankful, at least, that she wasn't in tears. He'd discovered that Holly's tears were the one thing that he couldn't handle well. "Whatever time I need? Honestly?"

He swallowed hard, and then answered her. "Honestly. It will be difficult for me to wait if it's much longer than a few weeks, but I'll do it."

Nothing could have surprised him more than her response. Laughing, she dashed around the desk and hugged him, leaning around the back of his chair to envelop him with her cheek pressed next to his in a warm embrace. "Don't worry, it won't be weeks. I can promise you that. Especially if you tell me I can have a little leeway around the office to do what I like. Could you give me that, for a week or so?"

Jake tried to regain his mental balance. This was so much more than he'd hoped for that now he was the one fighting emotions that didn't usually rise to the surface. "I think so, at least. I'll try. No, that's too unclear." He took a deep breath. "Yes, Holly, you can have as much leeway around the office as you need to do whatever it is you need to do to be ready to deepen our personal relationship. I've got to have faith in *you* through this process, too, not just God."

"Thanks, Jake." She kissed him on the cheek and released her embrace. "You are the best, you know that?"

Before he could answer she was out the door, and then popped her head back in. "Now I'm even more excited about getting things started. I'll start doing what I need to do, and I'll see you in the morning, okay?"

"It will be more like noon, but don't think I'm deserting you again," he told her. "I've got to go over to the courthouse for some last stuff with Rose."

"I should have remembered that. I took the message," she said, her smile a little wry. "Guess this conversation got me more mixed up than I thought. Do you want to plan on lunch, or will you be done that early?"

"Let's make a tentative plan, and if I'm going to be later, I'll call from Rose's office, all right?"

"That sounds good. See you then." She went back to her own desk and Jake could hear her humming. It was a wonderful sound, one he hoped he could hear much more of in the future.

"He said you could do anything you wanted? It must really be love," Sara teased Holly as they both stood in her office. "Seriously, though, is Jake going to totally lose it when he finds out you're switching jobs with me? What if I mess up?"

"I'll be just down the hall, Sara. You can ask me any questions you like, and I'll come in as often as you need me to translate any Jake-isms you have trouble with. Honestly, it won't be so bad," she said, as much to reassure herself as Sara. Holly was sure this was the right thing to do, but at the same time she was going to miss her days in the same office with Jake. They'd grown so comfortable working together.

She knew even more certainly that she would enjoy dating Jake more, and probably even marrying him if things worked out. The Jake Montgomery that she'd seen for the last few weeks looked like a man she could think about marrying. What an amazing transformation. But then, Holly reminded herself, they served an amazing God.

"I'm planning to have lunch with Jake today, and I'll break the news to him that way. I'm also going to put everything in writing, just to make it all legal and tidy for the bureau," Holly said. "In fact, I've been working on the letter on my computer, and once I hear from Jake and get ready to go to lunch, I'll print it out and leave a copy on his desk, and drop off one for you."

"I'm excited about this," Sara said. "A little nervous and scared, but excited, too. If anybody can mentor me into trying to decide whether or not to go for the next step and apply to be an agent, it would be Jake. I'm afraid that Bob and Donna just don't see me as agent material."

Holly had to admit that her friend's desire, when she'd shared it with her, had surprised her too, but she could imagine Sara making it through the rigorous training and doing it well. "It could happen," she told her. "Now go make sure everything's organized for me so that I can take over your job on Monday, and I'll see you soon with that letter."

"Great. I'll get to it." Sara had a definite bounce to her step when she left the room, and Holly found herself humming again as she worked, an indicator of her happiness with this whole decision.

It didn't take long to get everything in shape so that Sara could walk in on Monday and replace her. She hoped Jake truly meant what he'd said about letting her do whatever she wanted. This might not be what he had in mind, but Holly had to believe that once he knew the purpose behind her decision he'd be happy.

As if he knew she was thinking about him, the phone rang and it was Jake on the other end. "Hi, there. It looks like I'm on track to be done here soon. Do you want to meet me at the Stagecoach in thirty minutes? I'd come back to get you, but I'd be afraid we'd get tied up in the lunch rush that way."

"I can meet you there. We have plenty to talk about during lunch," she said.

"I can hardly wait. See you then," Jake said, his intimate tone of voice making her cheeks flush.

Holly hung up the phone and went straight to her computer, called up the letter she'd told Sara about and printed out two copies.

Naturally the printer chose this time to jam, and she spent ten precious minutes untangling the paper, putting fresh stock in and finally printing out the copies she needed. In more of a hurry now, she took the first copy, signed it with a flourish and put it in the middle of Jake's empty desk.

She shut down her computer and the offending printer, deciding she wouldn't miss that particular thing about this office at all. Jotting a couple sentences on a sticky note about the printer's quirks, she stuck it on the letter. Picking up the letter and her coat and purse, she flipped off the office lights and headed down to Sara's office to explain the awful machine and give her friend the letter before heading off to the lunch that would start a new phase in her life with Jake.

"Have a good time at lunch. Are you doing anything special tonight?" Sara asked a few minutes later. It took a moment for it to dawn on Holly that it was New Year's Eve.

"I honestly hadn't planned anything," she admitted. "I'd been so focused on this since yesterday that it slipped my mind. The church has a games night usually with all kinds of board games and popcorn, and silly paper hats for midnight. But I'm not sure I can see Jake agreeing to that. I have a feeling he's used to a different kind of New Year's Eve party." Even as she said that, Holly thought that the new Jake might be just as happy at Good Shepherd wearing a funny hat. She'd have to mention it at lunch and see.

She looked at her watch, surprised at how much time had passed while she explained the printer to Sara. "I really have to go now, anyway. If I don't leave soon, I'll be late and we'll have to wait for a table at the café. Besides, I'm parked out on the overflow lot outside instead of in the garage, and it's hard to get out of there this time of day."

"Go on, then. See you later. And Holly, thank you so much for giving me this chance."

"It's a chance for both of us," Holly said, smiling. "I'll see you Monday."

She went to the elevator, focused now on getting to the café the quickest way possible so that she could arrive before Jake and secure a table before everything filled up.

She sprang out of the elevator, slipping her coat on and heading out the front door of the building, her keys in hand. Holly could see her Jeep in the lot ahead of her when someone grabbed her elbow roughly. "I thought you'd never leave that building alone again," he said in a growl. "Now walk to your truck and get in. No screaming. I have a gun and I'll use it, understand?"

Holly's heart was beating so fast she could barely stand upright, much less think about making noise. Nodding, she went exactly where the man was steering her. While she walked across the lot she wondered how she could possibly get word to Jake or to anyone else that they'd been wrong all along about the man making their lives miserable. The stranger who had been stalking them wasn't working for Barclay. It was Victor Convy. He must have learned a few things in prison, because he wasn't giving her a chance to escape. He forced Holly into the passenger side of the Jeep and through to the driver's side where he pulled out a set of handcuffs. Smiling coldly he cuffed one of her wrists to the steering wheel. "Now we're going on a trip. I still have the gun, so don't try anything."

Holly wasn't sure what she could try while handcuffed to the wheel. She forced herself to concentrate and attempt to stay calm. It was a losing battle, but one she knew she had to keep fighting if she wanted to see Jake, or anyone else she cared about, again.

Chapter Twelve

I should call Holly again, Jake thought as he stood in front of the court documents section near the district attorney's office. When he'd called before, he thought this would be a two-minute stop on his way out of the building. Now it looked like it would be ten or fifteen minutes at least before he could sign the forms that Rose had told him to finish before he left.

Before the clerk could find the necessary paperwork, there was a flurry of activity behind them. Jake turned to see Alistair Barclay being escorted through the hall. He expected the man to ignore him, but to Jake's surprise Barclay stopped with his guard and looked at him. "You're Montgomery. That computer expert. Nasty bit of good work you did, I have to admit."

"No thanks to you. You're lucky I didn't press additional charges," Jake said, unable to keep silent.

"I have no idea what you're talking about," Barclay said blandly.

"Of course you don't. That guy who nearly ran down my assistant was working for somebody else altogether."

Barclay's eyes widened. "That's absurd. Surely you don't think I would have ordered something like that? I'd already been charged with enough. No sense to add something as unnecessary as manslaughter. To be honest, I didn't think you were good enough to break the code." The sneer he finished with was more the expression Jake expected from Barclay.

"Have it your way," Jake said with a shrug. It didn't matter that much. He and Holly were both safe, and Barclay was going to prison for a long time. Another charge now wouldn't keep him there that much longer and there was no way to prove anything, now that the guy doing the dirty work had slipped back into the woodwork.

The clerk still hadn't found the right paperwork and Jake was getting anxious. He was going to be late for lunch and it was the last thing he wanted to do. Suddenly Rose D'Arcy was next to him. "Forget about the paperwork. You need to go back to the office now. This minute."

Her tense expression made Jake wary. "Why? Half an hour ago you said this was vital."

"Well, I've found something more important. I

just got a call back from the Ohio Department of Corrections. I don't know why we didn't know before this, but Convy was paroled almost a month ago. And to make matters worse, his parole officer hasn't seen him in more than three weeks."

Her expression said this wasn't the end of the story. "What else?" Jake prompted.

"They talked to his last cellmate yesterday. He said Convy had talked a lot about going to Colorado when he got out. Something about evening the score."

Jake felt a chill up his spine. He pulled out his phone and called Holly's cell phone. It was turned off. "Maybe she's already at the café," he said. "I'm heading back to the office to try and catch her if she's there. You call Lidia at the café and see if Holly's there. I hope and pray she is." Just knowing that their mystery assailant could be the man who had gone to prison for Holly's rape gave him a terrible feeling.

He made the drive from the courthouse to the FBI office in record time. When he got there, he didn't even have to go inside before he started to panic. Outside on the sidewalk, a uniformed Colorado Springs police officer was talking to Sara Phelps. "Jake, you're here. Something awful just happened to Holly, and this guy won't take me seriously."

"All you're telling me is that you think you saw your friend get into her own car with a man you don't know. Do you know everybody that Ms., uh, Vance is friends with?"

"There's reason for concern here," Jake barked. "What did he look like?" he asked Sara, ignoring the officer's protests about who was running this investigation.

"Brown hair, in his thirties, maybe, medium height. Pretty nondescript. I was just coming out to tell Holly she hadn't signed the copy of a letter she gave me, when I saw this man steering her to the Jeep. He had her by the elbow, and it didn't look friendly. He pushed her in the passenger side of the vehicle, and then they took off." Sara, Jake thought, was observant enough to do this officer's job better than he was doing it himself.

"Could he have had a gun?" Jake was praying he wouldn't get the answer he expected.

Sara nodded. "I think he did, even though I didn't see it. Holly wouldn't have gone with a stranger like that unless he was armed."

"If you really think this is something, let me take the license number of Ms. Vance's vehicle, and get information on which way they went," the officer said.

"You'll do that, and we'll do more, immediately. Because I *know* this is something," Jake said. He pulled out his cell phone again, calling a number from his address list.

"Peter? It's Jake. That tracker you gave me? We

need to start tracing it now." Of all the times Jake had been glad to be friends with Peter Vance, he thought he had never been as glad as now. And he was especially glad that his old friend was back in Colorado Springs, having joined his brother in his security firm.

"Putting a tracker on somebody's car isn't legal without a court order, or at least their knowledge," the police officer said, as if that was going to be news to an FBI agent.

Jake closed his phone. "I didn't put it on for evidence. I put it on in case we needed to save a life. And it looks like now we do, because the man who abducted Holly has no intention of leaving her alive." He willed his voice not to shake as he admitted what terrified him now. He wondered if prayer came naturally enough to him yet that he could pray and work at the same time. He was about to find out, because he was ready to use every resource he had to find Holly before Convy hurt her again.

The farther out Highway 24 Convy forced her to drive, the more worried Holly got. Unless they went all the way to Cripple Creek near the ranch, nobody would be looking out here for her. Of course it would be hours before anybody would be looking for her, period. Once she didn't show up for lunch, Jake would wonder where she went, but no one would expect this.

Her heart sank even further when Convy ordered her off the highway at Manitou Springs. There were so many places out here where side roads could lead to relatively isolated territory as easily as they could a subdivision or a tourist attraction. And Convy seemed to have scouted out the area, because in a matter of moments they were driving on a narrow strip of asphalt that could hardly be called a road.

"Pull off there." He gestured with his gun hand at a break in the fence line. Another couple minutes of driving and they were surrounded by trees on a bluff that looked as remote as anywhere Holly had ever been. She looked around, wondering if she'd ever see another place.

Once the car stopped, Convy confiscated the keys and released Holly's wrist from the wheel. She looked for a chance to bolt, but he always had the gun trained on her. Stumbling along, they headed for the thickest growth of pine trees. When they reached it, Convy halted her and Holly fought her emotions so that she wouldn't break down. "Please...I want a chance to pray."

"Oh, you can pray all you want, for all the good it will do you. I stopped that nonsense a long time ago, but if you want to spend your last few hours that way, be my guest." His voice chilled her with its matter-of-fact tone.

"I would have thought prayer would be a comfort

in prison," she said, trying to keep him talking about faith. She'd gone to plenty of seminars the Bureau held, and keeping your assailant or abductor talking almost always made him focus on the fact that you were a human being. Holly prayed that Convy still thought of people as special.

"There are no comforts in prison, especially when the other people there think you're a rapist. The only thing that could have been worse on me was if I'd been convicted of messing with little kids," he said. "And it's all your fault, you and those high, phony morals of yours. Take off your coat," he barked abruptly, making Holly question his sanity with his quick change of topic.

She didn't argue. Sliding off her right sleeve was difficult, because the handcuffs still dangled from her wrist, but she complied. He tossed the garment away from her, and then working quickly, snapped the cuffs so both of her wrists were shackled. Pushing her roughly against the nearest tree, he pulled a length of rope out of the backpack he'd been dragging along since he got into Holly's Jeep. Soon she was bound to the tree firmly at the shoulders, waist and thighs.

"I should have left you free a little longer, to share one last gift with you," he taunted. "But if I leave any DNA they'll link me to your death, instead of thinking it's just the tragic suicide of a troubled young woman. Your church buddies will say bad things about you, won't they, Holly? I went to church long enough to know that suicide is a bad thing."

Holly shivered uncontrollably now, between the evil of Convy's ranting and the cold penetrating her body. "They'll find us before I freeze to death or you untie me, Victor. And when they do you'll go back to jail for good. You'll spend the rest of your life there unless you let me go now."

"I can't let you go. The only thing that kept me alive and sane in that place was thinking about what I'd do to you once I got out. And nobody's going to find you out here."

She was so afraid that he was right. "Aren't they looking for you anyway?"

He gave a mirthless laugh. "Not yet. I'm out on parole, Holly. You're looking at a model prisoner."

She wanted to tell him that she was looking at a horrible person, far from a model of any good behavior, but it would only make him angrier. Besides, she reminded herself, everybody is redeemable in the eyes of the Lord, even people as far gone as Victor Convy. It was difficult for her to imagine Convy as redeemable right now, but she knew that God did.

She felt her body sag against the ropes and realized that she was beginning to lose focus, maybe even consciousness now. Holly could hear Convy talking to her, and knew that while she struggled for consciousness, he'd been talking for a while. "It took a while to trace you, too. There are a lot of Vances out there, and you don't have a phone listing in your own name, or any Internet accounts, anything like that."

"So how did you find me?" Holly pressed her back against the tree, trying to make less of a target for the wind.

"I got a hint about where you might be by reading my own trial transcripts. It took ten or twelve times going over them before I picked up your one brief reference to being from Colorado. Even then it took another six months to find you. They don't give prisoners nearly enough unrestricted computer use."

Convy's grin was feral, bordering on crazed. Holly tried once more to make peace with the fact that she might not leave this place alive. It didn't seem right or fair, especially if Convy's plan worked and she appeared to be a suicide. Putting that thought aside, Holly willed herself not to cry and chill her body even further. She focused on the fact that whatever happened, Convy would eventually answer to a higher judge than the court system. Right now it was all she could do not to lose consciousness. Convy's voice droned on while Holly struggled to keep alert.

"You should wait for the local cops to catch up with you." Travis Vance's voice was sharp in Jake's

ear, and even though the man couldn't see him answering, Jake shook his head.

"That will take too long. Besides, we have a suspected abduction by a possibly armed and dangerous
felon. There are reasons for FBI presence."

"Yeah, well it ought to be another agent providing that presence," Travis Vance growled. "You're too
close to this one, Jake."

"Just like you backed off without argument when
it was Tricia in danger," Jake said, almost sorry he'd
said that when the words were out. Still, he would
argue any way he could to stay right where he was.
"According to your tracer, are they still stopped off
of Highway 24 somewhere?"

"That or he found the tracer."

"Not likely."

"I know. Looking at the maps, there's only one
road that leads in to where they should be." Travis
kept directing Jake up a narrow county road, then up
a track barely a lane wide. Suddenly Jake could spot
the Jeep up ahead. He cut the engine to the Escalade
and got out as quietly as possible.

"Thanks buddy. I owe you a big one. Tell Manitou Springs and Colorado Springs exactly where I
am, and that I'm going in now."

Jake could hear Travis sputter. "Oh, no. You wait
for backup, Montgomery. No Lone Ranger moves,
not even for Holly."

"Sorry, you're breaking up. So far out here, I can't hear you," Jake lied, taking off the headset and disconnecting it as he heard Travis sputter.

He knew what the right procedure was. He knew enough to wait for backup. But the woman he loved was in danger, and there wasn't time to wait for backup. They'd be here soon enough anyway, to clean up after him.

Jake tried to stay behind trees as much as possible, gun drawn, listening for sounds that would indicate that Holly and Convy were here somewhere near the Jeep. Moving without noise wasn't easy here. The underbrush rustled, and there were sticks on the ground ready to snap under an unwary foot. Finally he could hear one voice droning on. It was deeper, male. Jake couldn't hear anybody answering in return, but surely Convy wouldn't be talking like that if Holly was…not here. He couldn't even bear to think about the possibility.

He was moving more slowly now, aware of his breathing and every little noise. He wasn't close enough to get a shot at Convy yet, but he could see Holly. She was tied to a pine, but although her head was sagging to one side, there were no signs of blood, and she definitely seemed alive. Jake could hear her rouse herself and say something to Convy. It gave him hope that all of this could turn out okay.

Gun out in front of him again, he got ready to

move in on Convy. First he listened for more vehicles coming up the road, but there was nothing. The only sound besides Convy was an insistent bird somewhere nearby. Jake wondered for a moment what kind of bird would be here this late in the year, and then there was the distinct click of an automatic pistol slide.

Eight feet to his left a tall, dark man dressed in black materialized, a pistol much like his own at the ready. "What's going on?" Jake said with as little breath as possible. He'd never thought about Convy having a partner, and certainly not one as suave as Alessandro Donato.

In a flash the man was close enough to whisper his answer. "Let's just say I, too, am interested in my cousin Travis's toys. When this one activated I followed it." He gave a wordless, Mediterranean shrug. "You look like you could use help."

"How do I know you're on my side?"

"I'm certainly not on *his*," was the enigmatic answer. It was enough for now. Motioning for Donato to stay put, Jake noticed that Convy seemed to be silent.

"Who's out there?" Convy called. "I hear you. Come out with your hands up or I shoot the girl."

Jake took a deep breath. "Jake Montgomery, FBI. Convy, you're surrounded. Drop the gun."

"No. If I'm surrounded, come out and prove it," Convy said. "All of you."

Jake motioned for Donato to stay behind and silent. Then he walked toward the clearing, gun stretched out in his open palm. "Okay, you've got me. I followed you from the lot. But I alerted Colorado Springs and Manitou Springs on the way, and the rest will be here in a minute. So drop the gun, Convy, and get ready to surrender."

The small clearing was empty except for Holly. Jake scanned the bushes, wondering where Convy had gotten to. A blur of movement too close to him to dodge all the way was the last thing Jake saw before something hard came down near his right temple. Light flashed in front of his eyes and he sank to his knees.

Chapter Thirteen

When Convy knocked Jake out, Holly didn't know whether to laugh or cry. She knew Jake well enough by now to figure his claim to have backup was a bluff. Once he'd gotten wind of where she was, he'd probably gone off alone. So here he was, by himself, ready to save her. It proved to her, beyond a doubt, that he loved her. But it also said that he'd let love get the better of the instincts that usually made him a good special agent. Now they were both in trouble, maybe worse off than she'd been the moment before. She prayed that he'd let the police know where he was going.

At least Convy didn't shoot him right away. Kicking the gun far away from Jake, he rolled Jake on his back and pulled another length of rope out of his backpack. He was muttering to himself now, and

Holly could catch bits and phrases, like "I knew he was lying" and "but killing a cop is certain death" that at least gave her hope that Convy was still sane enough to know the consequences that harming Jake could have.

Since Jake was unable to do anything, it was up to her now to keep Convy busy until help came. "He wouldn't have moved in unless backup was at least closing in," Holly said, forcing the words between chattering teeth. She was trying to think as clearly as possible, searching for the right words to get Convy to do as little damage as possible. Maybe he'd even clear out if he got panicked enough. With luck he'd run into the police that she knew couldn't be far away. "If you want to escape, you better leave now."

"I'll take my chances," he said, staring at her. "I still think he was bluffing. Your hotshot boss wouldn't wait for backup. I've got a while until anybody else shows up. Besides, while killing him has consequences I'd rather avoid, killing you is another story. I still want to do that. I just have to do it quicker."

Holly was shivering so hard now that it was uncontrollable. She couldn't talk much because of the tremors in her body. Convy seemed to be mulling things over. He looked down at the gun in his hand, and a horrid grin spread over his face.

For a moment Holly couldn't figure out what he

was doing when he went over near Jake, ignoring his prone body while he looked around in the grass and pine needles. When he picked up Jake's automatic with a gloved hand, Holly lost whatever reserve she had and started shouting at him. "No. Don't shoot me. Don't you use that gun!" Her words echoed through the trees, as she tried to convey to anyone who might be out there that the situation had suddenly gotten more desperate.

"Shut up. I don't want to. It won't look like a suicide anymore if I shoot you." He paused, considering the gun he now held. "Unless I shoot both of you with his gun." He was almost caressing the gun now, making Holly shiver. "That's what I can make it look like, some kind of lover's spat gone terribly wrong. Yeah, I can even close your hand around the gun and put your prints on it afterward."

He walked over to Holly, getting closer and closer to her while she screamed. This was not how she wanted her life, and Jake's, to end. As Convy stepped beside her and raised the gun, it flew from his hand and he dropped to the ground.

Holly quieted down, listening to Convy scream even louder than she had. He was on his knees, clutching his arm. A dark stain seemed to be spreading on the sleeve of his parka. *Someone had shot him!* This was all happening so fast it was hard for her to comprehend it. Just then a dark-clad man entered

the clearing behind Convy, who was in too much
pain to pay attention to anything but his arm. He was
also making too much noise to hear the man, which
worked in the stranger's favor.

Leaning over Convy, the man reached out and did
something from behind him that made Convy crum-
ple into a heap on the ground as the man stepped
neatly aside. He picked up Jake's gun where Convy
had dropped it. "There's another gun somewhere…
maybe in his pockets or his backpack," Holly called.
The stranger probed around Convy and his belong-
ing and came up with the other gun. As he straightened Holly got a look at his face, and with a shock
recognized Lidia's nephew Alessandro Donato.

"Did you kill him?" she asked as he sliced the
ropes that bound her to the tree.

"No, *bella,* he's not dead. Not even mortally
wounded, although I suspect he will soon wish he
were." Grabbing her coat, he wrapped it around her.
"But now I hear sirens. Jake's real backup must be
on the way, which means I need to leave. You'll apol-
ogize to him for my failure to stay around and…chat,
would you say?"

"That's one way to put it. But Alessandro, you
need to stay to do a whole lot more than just chat. I
don't know how badly Jake's hurt and Convy may
wake up and—"

He tipped one finger under her chin, and Holly

could see his sparkling dark eyes. "Jake will wake up before Convy, and I am afraid that it is impossible for me to stay. Explaining what I'm doing here would get terribly…inconvenient." He walked her over to where Jake still lay and helped her to sit down. "It will be all right. *Ciao, bella.*" And then he was gone, vanishing seconds before four or five officers in full protective gear, guns drawn, stormed the clearing.

So this was what a concussion felt like. Jake hadn't ever had the pleasure before, and was certain he never wanted to again. This was why he worked with computers instead of doing more dangerous field work. Computer experts were not expected to go out and get their heads bashed in. *Amazing what a guy does for love,* he thought, trying not to shake his head while he thought it. Just the mere *thought* of moving his head from side to side hurt.

At least they'd let him ride to Vance Memorial in the same ambulance as Holly. That was a good thing, because neither of them seemed to be ready to go anywhere without the other. At first when he started regaining consciousness, he was sure he was hallucinating, because he was on the ground and his head was in Holly's lap. And he had no memory of where he was or how he'd gotten there. In a couple moments, he remembered just enough about the previous events to know that the scene before had been far different. The last thing he remembered was charging the man who had Holly in the clearing, and seeing Holly tied to a tree.

There had been somebody with him, though. Who else had been there? Jake's aching head wasn't letting him clear his thoughts long enough to remember. When he tried, he just got more dizzy and queasy, without the memory coming through. That seemed to be a real aggravation for the police officers, because it was obvious fairly quickly that Jake had been out of commission for a while, yet someone had shot Convy and freed Holly. Two guns, his own and one that Holly said belonged to Convy, lay in the grass next to Holly, far from Convy's reach. It didn't all add up.

Convy hadn't been able to add anything, because he hadn't regained consciousness before being loaded into a separate ambulance, along with a Manitou Springs police officer to keep watch on him, for the trip to a local hospital. Jake didn't argue with them loading the other guy first, as he appeared worse off than either of them. He was bleeding from an apparent gunshot wound. "I didn't shoot him, did I?" Jake asked Holly quietly. He really hoped he hadn't shot anybody without remembering it.

"No, Jake. You didn't shoot him." She was still shivering a lot with his head in her lap, but she'd told him that he was helping keep her warm, so Jake had endured the shaking even though it made his head hurt worse. If he could have sat upright he would have changed their positions and held her in his arms to warm her more. But even Holly wouldn't let him sit up. So he went along with the paramedics, letting the second unit take him and Holly to Vance Memorial, along with a Colorado Springs officer for protection if they needed it.

Jake knew that the officer would also need full statements at some point. He wished him luck. Holly would be able to give them something sooner than he would. Apparently from what she had said earlier, she knew who else had been there with them and shot Convy. Jake hoped that he'd remember that eventually himself. Having a hole in his memory was a disturbing thing.

For now he was happy lying back on the gurney in a bay in the emergency room, trying hard not to move his head much. Movement meant pain. If he lay silent he could hear them working on Holly in the next bay. He'd promised her he wouldn't go any farther than he had to. In the ambulance they'd decided that she was unhurt as far as anyone could tell other than being deeply chilled. Jake suspected that if they hadn't found her and Convy when they did, another hour would have had her close to freezing to death, if Convy hadn't killed her some other way first. The thought made him shudder, which in turn made him feel hideously nauseated.

He was going to need something for the headache pain pretty soon. But for now Holly warranted the medical attention, and to get much himself he'd have to call someone away from her, which he wasn't ready to do. He'd have to feel much worse than he did right now to call attention to himself at her expense.

He could hear them explaining treatment to Holly, wrapping her in warming blankets and monitoring her temperature. She was answering back and sounded lucid, so that was a plus. Lying here still and quiet, listening to Holly's voice in the next bay was a comfort. They were both safe and warm, out of danger. There was so much to be thankful for here. Jake tried to list all the things he was thankful for; maybe it would keep him from dozing off. He remembered just enough first aid to know that dozing off was a bad thing in his situation, one the nurses would argue about once they came back in. Sure enough a minute later there was a stern-faced woman insisting he stay awake and talk to her. He agreed as best he could, and she even got him something for the pain. Sitting up enough to sip water with the pills wasn't fun, but he got them down, and the nurse kept him propped up at a forty-five-degree angle so she could look in his eyes and ask him all sorts of annoying questions.

"You're going to have quite a goose egg for a couple days. I need to send you over to X ray to make sure that guy didn't crack your skull when he gave you that concussion. What did he hit you with, anyway?"

"I have no idea. I just barely saw it coming," Jake said. "Whatever it was, I think I'm real lucky he wasn't more accurate."

"You can say that again," his nurse agreed. "Two inches forward at your temple and you'd be in surgery right now, *if* you made it to the hospital."

That sank in, making Jake feel queasy again, as he praised God for how well He had looked after him and Holly. Jake was beginning to have a vague memory of his companion before he'd charged Convy, but he told himself his memory couldn't be right on that one. Why would a guy like Donato be tracking Convy, or helping out the FBI? Only God knew, Jake decided, thinking that his new relationship so far with his Lord seemed to consist of the most improbable events possible. Holly had always said God was awesome. She hadn't ever told Jake that He had such a wicked sense of humor. Certainly God had a use for everybody, and Jake decided that many of those uses were far beyond his own understanding.

Holly sat in her cocoon of blankets sipping sweetened hot herbal tea. Her ordeal in the woods was beginning to feel like a bad dream. "How's Jake doing?" she asked the nurse writing on a chart next to her.

"He's all right. They sent him up to X ray to make sure he doesn't have any fractures to go with his concussion. If it's okay with the doctors, would you like us to wheel him in here when he's done?"

"That would be great," Holly said. The last few horrible hours made her certain that they had a lot to talk about and the sooner the better. "How long will it be before I could have something to eat?"

"You could have hot soup anytime," the nurse told her. "I can have a tray sent in if you'd like."

Holly agreed, and looked around for a clock. It was a shock when she saw that it was late in the afternoon. Once that registered, she thought of something else. "Before you get the soup, could I have a telephone? I need to call my mom." Working for the *Sentinel*, her mother might have caught wind of the commotion in Manitou Springs by now, and even though no names would be attached, she would worry.

Holly debated on how best to break things to her mother without getting her even more worried. After a moment's thought, she called Rose's cell phone. "Hi, it's Holly. I'm okay. We both are."

For once Rose seemed to be left wordless. "That's great. You actually got me praying for you," she finally admitted. Holly knew what a stretch that was for her cousin, and she grinned. "I've been listening to police radios. Was it Convy who got shot? And are you and Jake really okay? I heard two ambulances dispatched."

Her cousin was as sharp as ever. "Convy was shot," Holly said, "And Jake and I are both in the ER at Vance Memorial. That's why I'm calling, more than anything. I want you to go over to the newspaper office and tell my mom what's going on. But make sure she knows that I'm okay, just chilled. They're almost ready to let me go," Holly said, hoping that was the truth.

She sat back, thinking about things. "I guess we are going to need at least one more favor. Both of our cars are in Manitou Springs out in the middle of nowhere, and Jake won't be in any condition to drive any time soon. We're going to need a ride home from the hospital."

"I can arrange that one too," Rose said. "Peter and Travis Vance have already called me to pass on an update, and I'll let one of them know you'll need a ride."

"You're the best," Holly told her cousin, just in time to see Jake come into the bay still riding on his gurney.

"Hey, no fair," he said, his words slightly slurred as if he were in pain or medicated. "I thought I was the best."

"Well, you are, normally. But right now I'd say you're a touch under the weather and Rose just found us a ride home from this place." The orderly pushing Jake's gurney maneuvered it so that Holly could reach out and hold Jake's hand. He smiled a little dreamily. "They gave you something for the pain, didn't they?"

"Yep. It's starting to work, too. And guess what? I have a concussion but no skull fractures, so they're going to let me out of here tonight, too. Who did Rose get for taxi service?"

"Either Peter or Travis Vance," Holly told him.

The pressure of Jake's hand in hers was getting a little more lax. "Great. Tell her to make it Peter. That brand-new car he bought for Emily to tool around in since he came home has better shocks. Besides, there's something I need to ask him."

"Oh? What is that, Jake?" It was a little funny, watching Jake, normally intense and edgy, with his senses mellowed by pain medication and a hard day.

"Something personal," he said, arching one perfect eyebrow. "Before that, I need to ask you something even more personal. I've been thinking, Holly. I know I said I'd give you all the time you wanted before we started dating. And I still mean it. But after today, I'd say that dating is highly overrated."

"Oh?" It seemed to be the only answer she could keep making to Jake—handsome, wonderful Jake— without bursting out in giggles. "What do you mean by that?"

"Dating is so casual. And I have no desire for our relationship to be casual, not after today. Life is too short for casual things. Do you think when you're ready for something more that we could just skip the dating and go straight for an engagement?" His grip on her hand tightened, and his blue eyes cleared a bit, waiting for her answer.

"Yes. Definitely. I've been thinking the same thing, but I was afraid you'd think I'd gone around the bend after what I told you less than forty-eight hours ago."

Jake gave a dry laugh, and then winced when the movement must have hurt his head. "Yeah, well, life changes. Look how ours both changed in a day. Even before that, you've certainly changed mine so much in the last month that I can't imagine a life without you, Holly."

"You did the changing, Jake. You and God. I just got out of your way and let you change," she told him, leaning over to brush the softest of kisses on his uninjured temple. God had changed her, too, as He'd been working changes in Jake. It would take a while for her to come to grips with how much had changed, in such wonderful ways.

"So you'll marry me?" Jake didn't seem to believe her answer.

"I'll marry you. It will take a little while to plan the kind of wedding I suspect our families will want. But I'll marry you as soon as we can put it all together, Jake."

"Oh, we've got it all together, or at least God has

put it together for us," Jake said with a soft smile. "Now all we have to do is work out the details." And there, in the unlikeliest of settings on side-by-side hospital gurneys, they began doing just that.

Chapter Fourteen

Two months later

"Dearly beloved," Reverend Gabriel Dawson began, "we are gathered here together in the sight of God to join these couples in holy matrimony."

Couples. The thought made Holly's head spin, but then it had been spinning most of the time for about nine weeks now, and it wasn't likely to stop soon. Jake's question for Peter Vance on New Year's Eve had gained him an unexpected answer; instead of a best man, he'd ended up with a double wedding. Holly could still hear the ricochet conversation that went on in Peter's car that night. "Well, sure, I'll be more than happy to stand up for you, Jake, if you'll provide the same services for me. It will get me out of a jam, because I don't dare ask either of my brothers without hurting the other guy's feelings, and I wouldn't do that for the world," Peter had said.

"So have you got Good Shepherd booked already? When's the big day?" Jake asked. Holly could hear the wheels turning in his head.

"Two months from now, to give Emily and my mother time to plan. I was originally pushing for tonight in Las Vegas, but I'm kind of glad that didn't work out now, seeing as how you needed a ride."

Before Holly could stop them, the guys were planning a double wedding, oblivious to her suggestion that perhaps the women might want some say in this as well. Instead of backing off, Peter got Emily in on things right away, and the four of them ended up staying up all night in Jake's parents' living room, drinking ginger ale to ring in the New Year and plan a wedding. At some point Marilyn Vance and Peter's parents had joined the impromptu party, making it the strangest New Year's Eve Holly had ever spent anywhere. They'd even had a baby New Year in the person of Peter and Emily's soon-to-be adopted son Manuel, who had gotten passed around to everyone that night.

Right now baby Manuel was spending the wedding ceremony happily ensconced in his grandmother Lidia's arms, smiling and seeming to cheerfully wait his turn for the moment that Peter and Emily had built into their vows to have the baby blessed along with their renewed union. He was such an adorable little guy, and looked so cute in the little white suit his parents had dressed him in.

The church was filled with flowers, Vances and Montgomerys. Holly felt a little sorry for Emily's out-of-town family coming into this profusion of the two mixed families. There were less than a dozen of the Armstrong clan, and while everyone else was perfectly welcoming, Emily's relatives probably felt overwhelmed in the face of all the boisterous mayhem of the rest of this crew. The friends and cousins of Holly's age group had all grown up together in such a tight bunch that she suspected it would take days to explain all the private jokes and shared experiences to anyone from outside their circle.

Seeing so many of them here today brought such a special feeling to her wedding day. Before she walked up the aisle with Mike, Holly had been afraid she would be teary, but it didn't happen. There were so many warm, friendly faces between the back of the church and Jake waiting for her in front, all she could do was smile.

Gabriel Dawson was a wonderful preacher, and he used his skills to perfection on the talk to the two couples that became a sermon for the whole congregation on love and new beginnings and how we are new in Christ every day. In what seemed like a flash Holly was walking down the aisle again with Jake, both of them laughing as they looked behind them to see Manuel steal the spotlight from his parents, waving from his mother's arm as the three of them followed Holly and Jake.

Holly was sure that today might be the only time she'd see a white limousine fitted out with wedding flowers and a car seat at the same time. Still, it was so much fun to pile all five of them in for the trip to the Broadmoor. On the way over they had their own private celebration between the happy confusion of the receiving line at Good Shepherd and the upcoming reception. "I think Manuel has got the right idea," Peter said ruefully to Jake, watching his son sleep. "Do you think we've got time for a nap?"

"Not a chance. That photographer is going to be on us again the moment these car doors open. I think Emily's going to come at you with a comb again," Jake teased him.

At that Holly and Emily were both getting the giggles, trying to keep things quiet enough not to wake the baby. It was a struggle. Jake decided to help by kissing her to stifle the giggles. The trip to the Broadmoor had never gone so fast.

Jake looked around at the ballroom of the Broadmoor, filled with about two hundred of his closest friends and relations. It had started out with them wanting a small, simple wedding. So much for the plans he and Peter had tried to cook up weeks ago. Of course, once all the mothers got involved, things got out of hand quickly. At least the guys had gotten their way for half of the day's events. The ceremony had stayed as small as possible, and simple. Jake knew he would remember that forever, and treasure the glow on Holly's beautiful face as she came up the aisle toward him on her brother Mike's arm.

The reception had gotten larger and more festive every time his mother and Lidia Vance had gotten together, however. Everyone else involved had finally let these two old hands at social direction have their way with the party, once Holly and Emily set a few ground rules. The four women got along so well that planning the reception was never a problem.

He and Peter had ducked out of that planning as quickly as possible. "Our job for this part, my friend, is just to say 'yes, dear' and 'sounds great, Mom' once in a while to the right woman, and then head for the hills," Peter had said somewhere about the first week of January, and Jake found he had to agree with him. Since there was so much family overlap, and so many social commitments among their parents, all four members of the bridal couples had let the grooms' families host the reception. It wasn't traditional, but Jake had lost count of how many nontraditional things had happened in this courtship and wedding.

First there was the engagement before ever really

dating. Some of their friends were aghast at that, but it suited him and Holly just fine. As if she knew he was thinking about her, his beautiful wife turned from where she was talking to Lucia two tables away in the ballroom and beamed at him.

He joined her at Lucia's side, giving his bride a soft kiss on the cheek. "I missed you. You've been gone a whole five minutes."

"Well, you looked like you were busy talking to Travis and Tricia. What did they have to say to you?" Holly asked, eyes sparkling.

"I'll let her tell you herself," Jake said, unwilling to tell a secret.

"I knew it!" Holly crowed, taking his hand and going over to the table where her aunt and uncle and her Vance cousins sat. She let go of him long enough to hug Tricia as she stood up. "Congratulations! When are you due?"

"The end of September," Tricia said, smiling. "I thought you said you weren't going to tell her," she chided Jake.

"He didn't," Holly said, laughing. "I wondered earlier because you looked so happy. When he said he'd let you tell me what you three were talking about over here, that clinched it. I'm so happy for you." She hugged her again, and Jake wondered how long it would be before people were telling him the same thing.

Travis looked as thrilled as Tricia with upcoming parenthood. "Mom's going to be in her element." Lidia was nodding to agree with him, having over-heard the conversation. "For years she's been nag-ging all of us about grandbabies, and in the course of six months she's gone from none to four, if you count present and future."

"And I love it," Lidia crowed. "With the other changes we're talking about, I'm trying to convince Max that I need to cut back at the restaurant and have fun with the grandbabies instead. Amy already loves helping me bake cookies. She's going to be such a great big sister." Lidia patted the hand of her oldest granddaughter, who smiled back at her, un-willing to say anything in front of this many grown-ups looking at her.

Amy ducked her head shyly and turned to her mother, whispering something in her ear. "Of course. Don't go far," Jessica answered back, and Amy slid out of her seat and went over to the next table. There her friends Hannah and Sarah greeted her and the three children started a game of some kind.

Jake could hear the children playing together, and Susan's twin daughters were telling Amy something about "when we get our new baby brother," making Jake wonder if he should add Gabriel Dawson to the fraternity of expectant fathers around here. His wife Susan, the twins' mother, looked stunning as she watched her own girls and Amy, who all got down from the table now to play nearby.

It was so great to see the changes in Amy, Jake thought. The little girl had blossomed since Jessica had married Sam last year, and Sam's family had all surrounded the child with acceptance and love.

They were surrounding him the same way, Jake realized, coming to grips once again that his marriage today made all the Vances his family as well. Holly's aunt and uncle and cousins were his now, which made it clear just why the size of the dining room had mattered so much in the houses Holly and he had looked at for the last two months.

As if reading his mind on the subject, Holly leaned over and said, "Sam and Jessica are having Easter brunch. She wanted to do a holiday dinner before she got too far along to worry Sam. That's three weeks from tomorrow, so we'll be back from Hawaii by then. I figured we could do dinner with your folks later in the day."

"This married life is complicated," Jake told her, still grinning. "I'm glad I have such a competent person to walk me through it."

"It makes all the difference," Sam piped up, his arm around Jessica. She smiled at him and rolled her eyes, and Jake marveled again at how lovely she looked in the flowing silk pantsuit, her expanding waistline announcing her advancing pregnancy. He knew there had been this many expectant mothers around him in times past, but until now, when it was his friends and family he'd never paid attention.

"You'll be that beautiful when you're carrying our baby," he whispered to Holly as they made their way to the head table a few minutes later. She blushed all the way to the roots of her hair, which she'd left loose in heady waves. "You're so beautiful now, and every change in our life will only enhance that beauty."

She looked at him, brown eyes glowing with happiness. "That's the most wonderful thing you could have said, Jake. I think all women worry some if their husbands will still think they're attractive then, but seeing Jessica and Tricia today, I'll worry a whole lot less. They're both so gorgeous and so happy."

"That they are. We just seem to be surrounded by happy people," Jake said, catching his brother Adam's eye at that moment and exchanging a smile. Adam and Kate sat with his parents, probably discussing their upcoming return to Venezuela as part of a group starting a new clinic in a rural area. It wasn't the life he'd choose, but they reveled in it, and Jake couldn't be happier for them.

Around the room, the servers were circulating with bottles of sparkling apple juice, pouring glasses for the wedding toasts. Jake got the notes out of his pocket to praise Peter and Emily, and saw that Peter seemed to be doing the same, handing Manuel back to his wife so that he could manage an index card and a glass at the same time.

Peter spoke first and of course was far wittier than Jake ever expected to be himself. "I'd like to thank everyone for joining us today to welcome my wife Emily and my buddy Jake into the Vance family, and my cousin Holly into the Montgomery clan. Why do I feel like this is like *Romeo and Juliet,* without all the gory parts and the feuding families?" Laughter rippled around the room.

"Seriously, though, I couldn't think of a nicer couple to share the happiest day of my life with. Here's wishing many future blessings to my cousins and dear friends, Jake and Holly Montgomery." The applause only quieted when Jake rose to return the favor.

"Thank you, Peter. I have to give the credit and the glory to God for bringing me to where I am today, and I am so honored that Peter and Emily and Manuel let us share this special day with them. It is so wonderful to call the man I've always thought of as my best friend part of the family now, thanks to Holly's generosity in sharing her relatives. On that note I'd like to toast my new cousins, Peter and Emily Vance and wish them all the happiness in the world."

The toasts went on for a few moments, and then Jake, still standing, quieted the room. "I promised my father, and Peter's, that they could have a few words before we went on to cut the cake and do a few other things. So I'd appreciate you giving your attention to our illustrious mayor and his best friend. Guess this Montgomery and Vance tradition of friendship goes back a ways, huh, Dad?"

"That it does," Frank Montgomery said, standing in the middle of the room where Maxwell Vance was now beside him. "I want to thank the kids for letting us share their day so that our families and friends will be the first to know what the rest of the city will find out tomorrow."

"As you know, my focus as mayor during the last half of this term has been rooting out the source of the crime and drug problems that have plagued Colorado Springs. With the collapse of the Diablo crime syndicate, and prosecution of those involved in bringing drugs into our city via La Mano Oscura, I feel that part of my work is done. After two terms as the city's mayor, I won't be seeking reelection in May."

There was a murmur around the room, as some present started to speculate at what Jake already knew. "It's time for me to spend some quality time with Liza and our growing family, and maybe even improve my golf game, if that can be done. In our fight against crime and drugs in the city, one name came up again and again, and that was the Vance family. Folks around here say 'a Vance never forgets' and I'm sure that once I announce that I'm endorsing my friend Max Vance as Colorado Springs's next mayor, you also won't forget all the things he's already done to make this a great city."

There was a cheer that went up, and in the aftermath when people were surrounding the two men, Holly turned to Jake. "So that's what Aunt Lidia meant when she was talking about the other changes they were making. Maybe she and your mom can give each other some tips."

Jake smiled. "Right. Mom can tell her all about the perils of being the mayor's wife and all the public commitments, and your aunt can tell her how to deal with having a retired husband around to drive her crazy."

"They'll all be happy." Holly inclined her head to where the two couples were surrounded by their friends, all talking at once. "Look at them—they're all in their element. Do you think we'll be that way in forty years?"

"I hope so. If that's what God has in store for us, I'll treasure every day," Jake told her, kissing her soundly to prove the point. He treasured this day already, and planned to cherish every one God gave him with Holly from this moment on. *The best is yet to be,* Jake thought.

He could hardly wait.

* * * * *

Dear Reader,

I hope you enjoyed Holly and Jake's story. It was quite an experience to work with so many fine authors in this series of books about the Vance and Montgomery families and how they used their faith to fight evil. I suppose we all do that in a lesser way each day, without considering it much. So many days in the past six months have started out with knowing that my "sisters" in this project were encouraging me, or holding me up in a prayer. I'd like to thank all of them, Gail, Carol, Felicia, Kate and Cynthia, for all that they've brought into my life.

In addition, a book like this with multiple areas of research can't be completed without a great deal of help from folks in a variety of professions. I'd especially like to thank Nathan Lee and Karen Nicastro for their excellent help in guiding me through the legal system. Anything I got right was due to their expertise, and the errors are all mine.

I love hearing from my readers. You can contact me at: P.O. Box 1167, Thousand Oaks, CA 91358 or find me at www.lynnbulock.com.

Blessings,

Lynn Bulock

Love Inspired®

A MOTHER FOR CINDY

BY

MARGARET DALEY

Widow Jesse Bradshaw had her hands full with her young son, her doll-making business and a gaggle of pets. She couldn't imagine adding anything more to her already crowded life— until jaded Nick Blackburn and his daughter moved in next door. Jesse was all set to use her matchmaking skills to find a mate for the workaholic widower, but what would she do when she realized that she wanted to be little Cindy's mom?

THE LADIES OF SWEETWATER LAKE:
Like a wedding ring, this circle of friends is never ending.

Don't miss
A MOTHER FOR CINDY
On sale January 2005

Available at your favorite retail outlet.

www.SteepleHill.com   LIAMFCMD

Love Inspired

UNDERCOVER BLESSINGS

BY

DEB KASTNER

Returning to her childhood home was the only way Lily Montague could keep her injured child safe—little Abigail had witnessed a friend's kidnapping and was in danger. Kevin MacCormack, called "guardian angel" by the girl, was helping her daughter learn to walk again. But Lily didn't know the strong but gentle man was an undercover FBI agent, there to protect them both. When his secret was revealed, would it destroy the fragile bond that had formed between them?

Don't miss

UNDERCOVER BLESSINGS
On sale January 2005

Available at your favorite retail outlet.

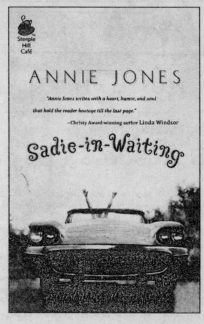

Take 2 inspirational love stories FREE!

PLUS get a FREE surprise gift!

Mail to Steeple Hill Reader Service™

In U.S.
3010 Walden Ave.
P.O. Box 1867
Buffalo, NY 14240-1867

In Canada
P.O. Box 609
Fort Erie, Ontario
L2A 5X3

YES! Please send me 2 free Love Inspired® novels and my free surprise gift. After receiving them, if I don't wish to receive anymore, I can return the shipping statement marked cancel. If I don't cancel, I will receive 4 brand-new novels every month, before they're available in stores! Bill me at the low price of $4.24 each in the U.S. and $4.74 each in Canada, plus 25¢ shipping and handling and applicable sales tax, if any*. That's the complete price and a savings of over 10% off the cover prices—quite a bargain! I understand that accepting the books and gift places me under no obligation ever to buy any books. I can always return a shipment and cancel at any time. Even if I never buy another book from Steeple Hill, the 2 free books and the surprise gift are mine to keep forever.

113 IDN DZ9M
313 IDN DZ9N

Name	(PLEASE PRINT)	
Address	Apt. No.	
City	State/Prov.	Zip/Postal Code

Not valid to current Love Inspired® subscribers.

Want to try two free books from another series?
Call 1-800-873-8635 or visit www.morefreebooks.com.

* Terms and prices are subject to change without notice. Sales tax applicable in New York. Canadian residents will be charged applicable provincial taxes and GST. All orders subject to approval. Offer limited to one per household.

® are registered trademarks owned and used by the trademark owner and or its licensee.

INTLI04R   ©2004 Steeple Hill

Love Inspired

TO HEAL A HEART

BY

ARLENE JAMES

Finding a handwritten letter at the airport offering
forgiveness to an unknown recipient put widowed
lawyer Mitch Sayer on a quest to uncover its
addressee…until he sat down next to Piper Wynne.
His lovely seatmate made him temporarily forget his
mission. After the flight, he kept running into Piper,
whose eyes hid painful secrets…including the fact
that the letter was written to her!

Don't miss

TO HEAL A HEART
On sale January 2005

Available at your favorite retail outlet.